Feisty Nuns

A MARY CATHERINE MAHONEY MYSTERY

Rita Moreau

Books by Rita Moreau

Bribing Saint Anthony

Nuns! Psychics! & Gypsies! OH NO!!

Feisty Nuns

The Russian & Aunt Sophia

Cover Design by George Moreau

First Edition – October 2016

Second Edition – October 2017

Printed in the United States of America

This book is dedicated to Kathryn Stosius (1918-2014) and Anna Kypriotis (1929-2015) two feisty women I'll never forget.

1

By way of introductions, my name is Mary Catherine Mahoney, MC for short. I was born and raised in Fish Camp, a small Florida town near State Road A1A, which stretches some 300 miles through oceanfront towns along the sometimes-blue Atlantic Ocean. State Road A1A extends from Amelia Island, just south of the Georgia state line, all the way to the southern tip of Key West. It's about a seven-hour drive…if you pay attention to the speed limit.

My friend and office manager, Velma, also grew up in Fish Camp, but not on the same block. She grew up in a black family, mostly female, large of body, but even larger of personality. They were church going, gospel singing women. Church was livelier for Velma than it was for me at St. Mary's.

My work, currently and for some time has been my life, and is dictated by my appointment book. Velma does her best to gauge the right amount of time to allot to my appointments. Unlike a doctor, I do not hold the power of life or death over my clients, so they are not always patient enough to sit in my office and wait. After all, most of my clients are filthy rich women who are used to people waiting on them. Many are also control freaks, which drives Velma and me batty during tax season.

Today one of my last appointments ran into overtime. The client was going through a big change of life: a divorce and her daughter and grandchildren moving back home. Not only was her personal life turned upside down, but so was her financial life. In her case, she was finding out that they did not have the money she thought; in fact, they were almost broke. The family had lived high, and she had not thought anything of their lavish spending. After all, she was married to a doctor. The prospect of being divorced is never pretty, but she was also now faced with the dim prospect of having to get a job, and she had no marketable skills.

Like so many others, she had dropped out of college to work while her husband finished medical school. She had spent her life as a full-time mother and a doctor's wife.

One day, after the children were grown and were starting lives of their own, her husband told her he wanted to do the same. She was looking for child support and alimony to get her through the transition. In that respect, I am like a doctor, my client's financial doctor. These appointments take a little longer. If nothing else, at these times I'm a good listener.

While I sat with my client, I heard my cell ding, and I looked down to see a text from Velma, who had only recently joined the twenty-first century, purchased a smartphone, and frequently used it to update me on the goings on in the front office. My next two appointments were now waiting for me in the tiny lobby of our office where Velma sits front and center. The text said that one had shown up early hoping to get squeezed in, and since she was already there she decided to sit and wait.

My attention went back to my current client, and then I heard the ding again. Velma's new text said the early bird was chatting on her cell and Velma was sure she was bent on calling everyone on her contact list. Geez!

Being psychic was no help when it came to setting up or managing appointments. Since I was finished with my current client, I escorted her out, while Velma escorted the next appointment into my office, and I also looked around surprised to find an empty lobby.

Velma returned to her command station and said,

"I convinced the early bird to step out and grab a bite to eat. It's the first time today I've had a minute to breathe," she said as she pulled out a small fan, plugged it in, and pointed it directly at her face and large bosom.

It was the middle of March, but the weather was unseasonably warm, even for Florida. It felt more like June than March. The snowbirds were happy, but not Velma, who was beginning to experience the joy of hot flashes.

As I headed back into my office, I watched as she picked up her cell to check for new text messages, mostly from her twin teenage daughters. It was a reminder that after work, her next job started: mom to twin girls, chauffeur, cook, and caregiver to her mother, Bessie.

The father of her girls, Rodeo, was out of town on a covert mission, and there was no communication. She had no idea where he was or who he worked for, but after almost 18 years she had finally made peace with that part of Rodeo's life. They were engaged and planning a wedding.

My next appointment went smoothly, no major life changes. As I worked on that client's return, I half listened to her small talk about the goings on in the life of a wealthy socialite. The various charities and social events she headed and the big trip she was taking next, a cruise around the world. I finished up her tax return, said my goodbyes, and escorted her out the front door of my office.

I turned around to see Velma looking out the window for my next appointment, the one who had shown up early with the hopes of being squeezed in, but she was nowhere to be found.

"She went out for a bite to eat about an hour ago and called me to say she was going to do some shopping. She should be back any minute now, which will make her late for her original appointment," Velma said rolling her eyes.

"Well, at least she is my last appointment for the day," I said. Velma gave me that look that said she wasn't my last appointment for the day.

"Velma, you didn't book me for another appointment, did you? At this rate, we'll both be here until midnight, and we have appointments starting early tomorrow morning."

"I had no choice," Velma said.

"Velma, who did you book that you, of all people, could not say no to?"

"Sister Hildegard. She just called and said they were coming over on the afternoon Greyhound bus. I'm surprised we don't hear the clackity-clack of their black pumps coming down the sidewalk. They should be here soon. They said they had to talk to you right away, something about an audit."

"Sister Hildegard? An audit? Is the IRS auditing nuns now?"

Velma then shrugged her shoulders as my next appointment, the early bird now late, came through the front door.

We greeted her, and I escorted her back to my office along with several large Nordstrom shopping bags, which I knew were full of expensive boxes and tax receipts. Looking at their boxes actually helped me to keep up with the latest fashion trends since I was not a fashionista.

I sat the client down, excused myself, and went back up front to Velma's desk. Something bothered me about the Sister Hildegard thing. "I don't believe this is happening again. See if you can get my Aunt Sophia on the phone. Try to find out what this is all about, so we at least have a heads up on those nuns."

"Already tried, not home, got their voice mail. You want me to try the public access TV studio?"

"No," I said as I resigned myself to the inevitable and headed back to my client, who was already chatting on her cell.

I knew something was coming, like a storm you could see off in the horizon. I had dreamt about it last night as I walked in Dreamland, a place a gypsy once told me was located between the visible and invisible world. It was only a matter of time.

2

I found myself seated at my desk in my office surrounded by a flock of nuns. I had first met these nuns a few months back when they showed up with my Aunt Sophia. Their arrival came with a direct order to find a long-lost jewel, which possessed a special power. I found it, but the road to discovery hadn't been easy. It did, however, force me to accept my psychic power—finally.

Their ringleader was Sister Hildegard. Her formal title is Mother Superior. She sat directly across from me instead of sitting in my seat, which is where I found her the first day I met her. Next to her was her right-hand gal and sidekick, Sister Matilda. Their eyes (and the ones in the back of their heads) were laser focused on me. They made sure that Velma joined us, and sat her down between the two of them.

Being a large, black woman, sitting between two nuns dressed in their full habits was causing Velma great discomfort, which was highly unusual for her. The other three nuns who rounded out the entourage were seated to my left and were busy being quiet.

Wanting to get to the heart of the matter as quickly as possible, I asked, "Sister Hildegard, as glad as I am to see you, what brings, ahem, all of you to my little office on such a beautiful day?"

"We are being audited," Sister Hildegard said. Like my mother, she didn't believe in small talk.

I shook my head, "Audited? By the IRS?"

"No, worse, by the Vatican," Sister Hildegard said. "And Bishop Michael is behind it."

"Bishop Michael?"

"Is the Pope Catholic? Yes, Bishop Michael," Sister Hildegard said, and then catching herself she added, "Rumor is he is getting close to that promotion to cardinal. So, we have started to call him 'Red Hat.'"

"Red Hat?"

"Cardinals are the *princes* of the church, appointed by the Pope," Sister Hildegard said with a touch of sarcasm.

Sister Matilda added, "Cardinals wear a red hat that looks like a beanie. Red is supposed to symbolize their readiness to spill their blood for the church. Like *that* would ever happen."

Velma and I had met Bishop Michael when I helped them find the long-lost jewel. He was rigidly conservative, a lawyer before he became a priest, and he was fond of debating theological and legalistic arguments. To his way of thinking, strict adherence to doctrine won out over mercy every time.

"I don't understand. I've never heard of an audit of nuns. What in the world for?" I said looking at Velma who just shook her head, rolled her eyes, pulled a small fan out of her bosom, and started fanning herself.

"Hot flashes, dear," Sister Matilda said, and before she could go any further on the topic of hot flashes and menopause, Sister

Hildegard's voice commanded our undivided attention.

"Sister Matilda, please explain how an audit of nuns by the Vatican works, and be quick about it." Sister Matilda looked at her and nodded her obedience.

"Yes, Mother Superior."

Sister Hildegard was, without a doubt, the tallest nun I had ever met. She easily could have played on a professional basketball team. Velma and I had both attended and survived parochial schools. Velma's mother had sent her to *Mary Help Us*, the all-girls Catholic high school in Fish Camp. The same high school I had attended about ten years earlier. Her mother thought that if she could isolate Velma from the opposite sex, she would stay on track to make it to the Olympics.

"It was a good plan that didn't work out," Bessie would say to her group of church ladies. "Praise the Lord." They would shake their heads in unison and respond, "Amen, sister, amen."

Sister Matilda was the opposite of Sister Hildegard, short and petite, but she carried herself with the same erect stature as Sister Hildegard. Sister Matilda was a history buff. Actually, she was a walking Wikipedia on almost any subject. The nuns at their convent did their best to avoid conversations with Sister Matilda that might lead to what they had dubbed *history time*.

"God forbid you ask her a question by accident," they would say to each other and make the sign of the cross.

I looked over at the three nuns sitting to my left, and I could see in their faces they knew what was coming. They settled into their chairs, and two of them made the sign of the cross and closed their eyes. Sister Matilda got up and glided to the middle of my office, center stage. We adjusted our seats and necks to give Sister Matilda our undivided attention. Velma's fan was fluttering at warp speed.

"The Vatican has appointed a group of American bishops to rein in the nuns of the United States. A cardinal high up in the

Vatican has convinced the Pope that American nuns have gone astray and fallen into serious doctrinal error. They want this addressed. We understand that the Cardinal tapped Bishop Michael for the job. The bishop has decided to start the audits close to home with our order, the Sisters of Saint Anthony."

"Holy Smoke," Velma said. "This is serious. I've heard that Bishop Michael has plans to make it all the way to Popedom."

"If he does well with these audits, he will be a shoo-in for promotion to cardinal and therefore, a contender when the time comes to choose the next pope," Sister Matilda said and walked over to give Velma a high five. She stopped cold when Sister Hildegard stood and clapped her hands.

"Sister *Matilda*," she said and paused while we all held our breath. "Do remember that there is a penalty for excessive celebration in the end zone. Please continue."

"Yes, Mother Superior," she said as she walked back to her invisible podium, and we all resumed normal breathing.

Sister Matilda along with her love of history had an equal love of sports. She had a great passion for football, college or NFL; it didn't matter. She could give you play by play along with the best sportscaster. That was the reason the nuns at the convent avoided her on Monday mornings during football season, especially if her teams played poorly.

Sister Matilda resumed her spot center stage, but then walked around the room, which required Velma and me to turn our necks to follow her movement. Sister Hildegard had gotten up and walked over to the back window of my office, overlooking the canal. She stood with her arms together and all ten toes tapping. She was calling on her patience. She knew whenever she gave Sister Matilda the floor, she would inevitably have to rein her in.

I closed my eyes and silently said a prayer to Saint Anthony; after all, these were his nuns. "Saint Anthony, Saint Anthony, please come down. Something is lost and needs to be found." That would be my sanity.

Saint Anthony is the saint you pray to when you've lost something. He doesn't care if you're Catholic or not. I knew him well; he was my mother's favorite saint. My mother had filled me in early in life about how to ask Saint Anthony for help.

Only she called it *Bribing Saint Anthony*. I once asked her where she came up with *Bribing Saint Anthony*. She turned to me and said, "Your husband, Theo." I didn't dare ask her anything further since that would have opened the door to a discussion about my ex-husband, Theo, who she absolutely adored.

I could hear her voice now as I sat looking at Sister Matilda.

"If you have a special request in your heart, then you pray to Saint Anthony. It's got to be something big, you don't want to waste his time. Say, for instance, maybe your only daughter getting married to a good man." Later, after Theo and I divorced she changed it to "Say, for instance, your only daughter staying married to a good man."

"MC, are you listening?" Sister Matilda said. She had been my third-grade teacher, so she knew exactly when to ask me that question.

I just nodded my head yes, up and down, and she continued.

"We received a letter from Red Hat's office telling us that the audits are necessary because the Vatican is concerned that some nuns are leaning toward what they call "radical feminist themes, incompatible with the Catholic faith."

"Really, like what?" Velma asked.

Sister Matilda looked over at Sister Hildegard still standing by the window in the back corner of my office.

"Well, let's see. They are a little ticked off, for one, that we may be challenging the all-male priesthood by pointing out the secondary role that nuns and, for that matter, all women play in the church," Sister

Hildegard said and nodded to Sister Matilda to continue.

"We are being referred to as those *feisty nuns*," Sister Matilda said as she continued. Velma and I looked at each other, and by the look on our faces, we certainly agreed that the term was appropriate.

"By way of background, the mission of the Sisters of Saint Anthony is to follow the path of our patron, Saint Anthony. He is more than the saint in charge of the lost and found. Sometimes in life, you might take a wrong turn and find yourself lost, and he is there to help you find your way home. The mission of the Sisters of Saint Anthony is to help those who have lost their way make it safely home," Sister Hildegard said with authority.

"Back to this audit," I said. "Does either Red Hat or the Vatican have the authority to tell the Sisters of Saint Anthony what to do like the IRS does in a tax audit?"

Sister Matilda went silent and then looked over to Sister Hildegard.

"Generally, religious orders are separate and independent of the local bishop and diocese. But, Bishop Michael seems to have forgotten that and to keep the peace we have tried not to remind him. However, now that he is under the wing of this powerful cardinal, it's not as clear. It could be argued that this gives him authority over our order of nuns since he is working for a cardinal who works for the pope," Sister Hildegard said.

"So, do the Sisters of Saint Anthony have to take orders from the Pope?" Velma asked.

Sister Matilda, still silent, continued to look to Sister Hildegard to answer these questions.

"We take our orders from God," Sister Hildegard said looking out the window at the water in the canal.

"We like to think of the Pope like one would think of the President. He is the commander in chief of the Catholic Church, but we may not always belong to his political party," Sister Hildegard said with a smile and then clapped her hands and gave Sister Matilda the cue to keep going.

"As both of you might recall, nuns played a vital role in the Catholic Church during the 1950s and 1960s. We ran schools, operated hospitals, and parishes were expanding. Today the number of nuns is dwindling, less than 50,000. Down from around 200,000 back in the glory days."

"Many American nuns no longer wear religious habits and have left convents to live independently. They have branched out into new lines of work. We are a small order of nuns, and we are not in a hurry to change our ways. We decided to keep our habits and the convent life."

"Why is that?" Velma asked.

Sister Matilda again looked to Sister Hildegard to answer that question.

"We chose to continue to wear our habits because we felt the habit was a strong symbol and part of our identity. Most of the nuns in the U.S. have chosen otherwise. Whether they or we made the right decision or not is still being debated," Sister Hildegard said.

"Aren't there nuns who are vocal and advocate for the poor and for social justice issues? Don't they call them 'Nuns on the Camper' or something like that?" Velma asked.

"There is a group of nuns that have been labeled by the media as the 'Nuns on the Camper' since they frequently drive an older Bluebird motorhome across the country and hold rallies. These sisters see advocating for social justice as acceptable. As a group, they are not shy and have even appeared before Congress. The leaders of the church, however, do not see it that way," Sister Matilda said.

"What do these audits have to do with that group?" I asked.

"We are not sure, but it's safe to say that the current leadership in the church is very conservative, so they would be happier if nuns were less vocal and disappeared back into the shadows where they used to be," Sister Hildegard said.

"So, the Nuns on the Camper are like Baptists preachers who go town to town and hold big tent revivals," Velma said.

"Why yes, that's one way to put it, Velma," Sister Matilda said with a smile.

I heard a noise coming from Sister Hildegard's direction. She was still standing by the window, and as I watched, I could see her habit rippling along the wooden floor. She was tap dancing in her black pumps.

"The Vatican thinks nuns in the U.S. are spending too much time on issues of poverty and social justice and not speaking out enough against abortion and same-sex marriage." Sister Matilda was now on a roll and about to continue merrily down that road when the tap dancing stopped. A loud clap came from Sister Hildegard.

"Get to the point, Sister Matilda. You're getting off track," Sister Hildegard said as she now began to pace from the window to my desk, then stopped right behind my chair and then paced back to the window. When she stopped behind me I could hear her whispering, "Mother of God, help me."

"Yes, Mother Superior," Sister Matilda said as she rolled her eyes upward and made the sign of the cross.

"It is not a secret amongst Catholic nuns that the male conservatives and traditionalist leaders of the Catholic Church would prefer to see nuns embracing a more conservative message."

"Like what?" Velma asked.

"Oh, like telling young women it's wrong for them to use contraceptives. Even if they are married," Sister Matilda added with an animated *what's up with that* look on her face.

"This is what is coming from the all-male leadership of the church, men who have never married and are allegedly celibate. We are losing our young women and men," Sister Hildegard interjected.

"They are so out of touch," Sister Matilda added.

"Sister Matilda, we have a bus to catch to get back to the convent," Sister Hildegard said giving her the signal to wrap it up and added a couple more claps in double time. Sister Matilda nodded okay, and then went right back to history time.

"The all-male leadership explains their stance by saying God revealed sacred truths to the pope and eventually it trickles down to the bishops, priests, and to the people. It's not for nuns, who are on the bottom rung, to question the all-male leadership on church doctrine. Those things are the way they are because God said so," Sister Matilda said pointing her pointer finger toward the heavens.

"I get it," Velma said. "It's pretty clear to me. The male dominated church would like you nuns to go back to being their workers. There was a time when they called that slavery."

Both Sister Hildegard and Sister Matilda looked at Velma, taken aback by her remark.

But then they looked at each other, made the sign of the cross, and nodded their heads like sister bobblehead dolls.

"I know the bishop has not been a friend of your order because of his conservative leanings, but until now and for the most part he has left your order alone. I'm wondering why he chose your order for his first audit," I said.

"It's like he plans to make a statement," Velma added.

Sister Hildegard looked at Sister Matilda and then said, "For years now I have guided our order of nuns along a path that attempts to keep us under the radar. Something has changed with the bishop. He has become bolder since he succeeded in aligning himself with this powerful cardinal and others who are close to the Pope. With their backing, he could make it very uncomfortable. He might even try to close us down."

"Close down the convent? I said. "Why? Can he do that?"

"Well, he can certainly try," Sister Hildegard said.

"The cardinal has the authority to remove our status as members of an officially approved religious community. Basically, he could kick our order out of the Catholic Church. The cardinal could make it very uncomfortable for us, especially since we are not as financially sound as we were in those glory days Sister Matilda spoke of."

"So, he would try to cut off your funding?" I asked.

"There is no funding," Sister Hildegard replied.

"No funding?" I asked.

"Wait a minute. Are you saying the Catholic Church does not support their nuns?" Velma said.

"That's exactly what I'm saying. Most Catholics have no idea that nuns fend for themselves financially. Many orders of nuns are disappearing. You might say the church is putting us out to pasture," Sister Hildegard said.

"Wow," Velma and I said in unison.

Sister Hildegard now walked over to Sister Matilda and gently guided her back to her seat. She took the stage,

"Thank you, Sister Matilda. MC, you are aware that some of the nuns within our order possess psychic abilities. It is a secret society within the order."

"Yes, I am very aware of that, Mother Superior," I said, again thinking back to the first time these Sisters of Saint Anthony paid me a visit.

"Of course, you are, dear. At times, we find our abilities are useful in furthering our mission as the Sisters of Saint Anthony. These abilities allow us to take our mission a step further."

"A step further," I said.

"Yes, as the Sisters of Saint Anthony we help those who are lost in the world, and sometimes we have to call on our psychic abilities. Let's just say it speeds up the process of assisting those lost souls who come to us for help. While we wait for our prayers to be answered, we look to our psychic abilities as a gift from God."

"It works much like a GPS," Sister Matilda piped in to offer a quick analogy. Sister Hildegard gave her an approving nod, which left Sister Matilda with a beaming smile on her face.

"Up until this audit business, the bishop has left us alone. A sort of 'don't ask and don't tell' relationship. But, as I said, the times are changing. He has become a real rock star amongst the conservative leaders of the church. Feisty nuns using psychic abilities to help their flock! Why, if this were to become public, his chances of becoming pope would be French toast. He'd be lucky to be demoted to altar boy. Since this bishop is blindly ambitious and has had his sights on becoming the first American pope, the last thing he would allow is a group of nuns in his diocese to stand in his way. I'm sure he views this audit as a way to rack up some points on the road to becoming pope. Closing down the order might be necessary, in his eyes, to become pope," Sister Hildegard said.

"We feel that this audit is just a first step. His brother Walther is also very powerful, and he is equally ambitious with his eyes set on eventually becoming president. According to the latest media, he is looking good to be nominated on the party's ticket as vice president. Can you imagine that? Katy, bar the door if one brother is president and the other is pope. It would be a powerful alliance. He could not afford to allow us to continue our works. We would be the skeleton in his closet."

"Goodness, it sounds serious," Velma said.

"It is serious. Our only hope is that there is a rumor that something is about to break at the highest administrative level of the church known as the Curia. There is some talk that, as a result, the current pope might even step down. The sisters are praying for a new pope from the more progressive side of church leadership. One who would not support the conservative leanings of current Pope Bernard and his gang of cardinals," Sister Hildegard said.

"We sisters have referred to them as Pope Benny and the Jets," Sister Matilda said.

"The world is not quite as black and white as the Vatican sees it. Down here in the trenches, it's gray, and on some days, it's covered in a heavy fog. It helps to clear the path when we use our psychic ability to help those who need to make some decisions on which way to go," Sister Hildegard said.

"MC, the sisters need your help with this audit."

"I understand," I said. "But how can I help you?"

"The Vatican has appointed a nun, Sister Clarissa, to assist the bishops, including Red Hat, with the audits here in the U.S. She has contacted us and asked for a meeting. We would like you to attend the meeting and represent the Sisters of Saint Anthony. Handle the matter, just like you do with your clients who are being audited by the IRS, easy breezy. Just think of Sister Clarissa as an IRS agent, but instead of representing the IRS she is representing the Vatican."

"But this is a little different," I said. "It's not the IRS. It's the Catholic Church. If you remember I am not as familiar with the laws of the church as I am with tax law."

"Yes, yes, we all know you slept through catechism, but you and Velma are the right ones to handle this audit. Trust me on this. Wait till you meet Sister Clarissa. You'll see what we mean. She is a Harvard graduated lawyer. You'll be right at home with her. She's a real pit bull if you know what I mean."

"Yeah, a real bitch," Sister Matilda said, as we three looked at her—stunned. "A female pit bull, just saying," she said shrugging her shoulders.

"Sister, you will spend some time in the chapel thinking over those unkind remarks," Sister Hildegard said. "And I will join you because you read my mind." She turned back to Velma and me and handed us a piece of paper she had retrieved from a hidden pocket in her habit.

"Here is the letter we received for the audit with a list of questions, which Sister Matilda and I have answered. You and Velma will attend the meeting with Sister Clarissa as our representative. If she asks you something you can't answer, look over at me. I'll either answer the question, or we can say we will get back to her on that, or whatever you say when you are dealing with those IRS agents," she said with a shrug of her very large shoulders.

"We'll also need your help delaying this audit for as long as possible. Our hope is that the pendulum will swing the other way, and this audit will die down and go away."

"I still don't understand auditing nuns," Velma said. "That's got to be bad press for the church."

"Well, it definitely serves to take the spotlight off of the real issues facing the church. I am sure you both have read about one scandal after another in the news. Horrendous deeds that have been swept under the rug by many bishops," Sister Hildegard said sternly.

"In other words, the nuns of the Catholic Church will become its scapegoats," Sister Matilda said.

"What rumors are you hearing about the Curia?" I asked, curious about what Sister Hildegard had mentioned.

Sister Hildegard's voice lowered an octave. "Yes, the Curia is like the house or the senate for the Catholic Church. The latest rumor is in your ballpark, MC. Supposedly there are some financial issues with the Vatican Bank. It's leaking to the press. One rumor swirling about is that this is the final straw, and it's so big it may lead to the pope stepping down,"

Sister Hildegard said, and then walked back and had a seat.

"The Vatican bank?" I asked.

"Right up your alley. Some talk is that it has to do with money laundering."

"Oh, really?"

"The Vatican Bank is very secretive. In fact, some would argue that it's the most secretive bank in the world. Most people are not even aware that the Vatican has a bank. It is beyond the reach of anyone except the pope. On occasion and in the hands of the wrong church leaders, its secrecy and power have been misused. It has been said that after World War II, it had cozy ties with the mafia and during the cold war was used in money laundering operations involving the CIA and the Catholic Church," Sister Matilda said.

"Whoa," I said.

"Yes, whoa indeed," Sister Hildegard said.

"Our Red Hat bishop has caught the eye of Pope Benny and the Jets. He was a lawyer on

Wall Street before he became a priest. He has a solid legal and financial background and is politically powerful. He is looking very attractive to that group as someone who could help with the Vatican Bank and other problems facing the church. Whatever is going on with the Vatican Bank, the male hierarchy of the church will do everything to hide it as they have done for eons. This audit may be a test to see how he handles himself."

"What is this cardinal's name, the one who is spearheading these audits?"

"His name is Cardinal Peter Sole. He is involved with the Vatican Secret Archives. He is the librarian."

"The Vatican Secret Archives?" I said.

Sister Hildegard shook her head side to side, and with a grimace on her face looked over at Sister Matilda, who was waiting patiently to launch into history time.

"Quick, Sister Matilda, if we miss the bus we will have to call an Uber cab."

"Yes, Mother Superior," Sister Matilda said as she popped up and stood behind her imaginary lectern.

"The Vatican Secret Archives are housed in a section of the Vatican Library. It serves as a place where the personal documents of all popes and thousands of other documents have been housed for over 400 years. It's not open to the public. It's not a place where anyone can walk in and have a look around. Scholars may apply for admittance, but they must be specific as to the purpose of their visit. There are limitations on what is available for viewing. No materials after 1939 are available to the public. Some even call it the Vatican's Hangar 51, because it may house evidence of alien life."

"Really," Velma and I said at the same moment.

"Yes, the Vatican takes this life beyond our planet very seriously. All church conspiracy theories tie back to the Vatican Secret Archives."

Sister Hildegard looked down at her watch and signaled to everyone that they were ready to leave.

"Enough with the aliens and conspiracy theories, Sister Matilda, we've got to go. We have to run to catch the last Greyhound bus."

Sister Hildegard headed toward the lobby of my office, and Sister Matilda and the three sisters who had been sitting quietly jumped up and followed Sister Hildegard and Sister Matilda.

Velma and I walked along with the group, and as they were heading out the front door Sister Hildegard turned to me and said,

"One more thing, be very careful. We think Sister Clarissa has some unique powers of her own. That is why she makes such a great lawyer. As Sister Matilda said, she is a bitch, but she is also a very clever woman. And, like the Bishop, she is very ambitious, and that ambition clouds her judgment."

"Dang," I said to Velma as we watched them clackity-clack their way down the street and disappear around a corner.

"The nuns on the Greyhound bus strike again."

3

*Could you come by my house this afternoon?
I have something important I need to talk
over with you.*

I put my cell down after reading the text from
my client Jennifer Stone. I don't usually
make house calls, but for Jennifer, I could
make an exception. With her big house that
sits facing the Atlantic Ocean, getting out of
the office for a change of scenery was calling
my name. Velma had already left for the day,
and I always felt a little out of sorts when she
was not up front guarding the entrance to my
office.

After the meeting yesterday with Sisters
Hildegard and Matilda, I was leery about who
might walk into my office. The sisters had
not wasted any time. Velma told me that the
bishop's secretary had called and asked that I
give him a call. He wanted to discuss the
audit of the Sisters of Saint Anthony. Sister

Matilda had also called to tell us that he was livid. Right now, a fresh ocean breeze was calling me while I put off the call to the bishop. It wasn't going to be pleasant when he heard what I had to say.

I quickly texted Jennifer back:

I will be there in about an hour.

To which she replied:

Awesome, I'll put out some wine to chill.

The reply text was also followed by a couple of happy face images, which I haven't figured out how to do yet.

I got into my car, headed down US 1, cut over to A1A, and found myself in bumper to bumper snowbird traffic. It was winter when everyone from Canada and parts north relocates to Florida.

While driving, I went over what I knew about Jennifer Stone. She was the richest woman in Fish Camp and maybe the state of Florida. She had been born with both beauty and brains, and she had used them both to amass her fortune. Jennifer seemed like the perfect trophy wife: trim, blond, buxom, and a natural ability to say the right thing at the right time, a real social butterfly.

She could put a spell on any man within her radar range and at the same time engage the man's wife in conversation as if they had been lifelong friends. This made her the perfect fundraiser for charities and for those running for political office. I'm sure when she gets a little older she could make a run for governor. For now, she was looking for me to provide tax guidance for the accumulation of cash and other assets she had already acquired upon the dissolution of several marriages.

She also was very superstitious and relied on my Aunt Sophia to read the family fortune-telling cards. Aunt Sophia was the first person she talked to before making any important decision. This, at times, required calling my Aunt Sophia before I could move forward on Jennifer's tax planning. I wasn't alone; her stockbrokers and attorneys knew the drill, too.

After graduating from high school, Jennifer took off for Nashville along with a suitcase of dreams. She had hoped to become a country music star. Somewhere along the way she got on the wrong bus and missed Nashville, and landed in Las Vegas instead.

She landed a couple of singing gigs, where she met and married the first of her wealthy husbands looking for trophy wives.

Jennifer fit the part well, and the rest is history. Her last husband was rumored to be part mafia/part hedge fund owner. Upon the dissolution of that marriage, she kept the mansion right on A1A facing the Atlantic Ocean.

She also reconnected with her high school sweetheart, Joe (her soul mate according to my Aunt Sophia). Jennifer and Joe have had an on-again, off-again relationship and Jennifer controlled the remote. She wasn't ready to settle down with Joe to become a wife and mother, so Joe waited.

Lately, though, my Aunt Anna, who knew all the latest gossip, told me that Joe was becoming impatient. I wondered if this was what Jennifer wanted to talk about.

When I got to Jennifer's mansion, I turned into the driveway, made my way to near the front door, and parked right behind her red, convertible Corvette, which had its top down. I drive an older Ford Explorer, but so far, it has never let me down. And as long as it starts and gets me where I'm going, I'll probably continue to resist buying a new car.

From the road, Jennifer's mansion looks like a hotel because it is the size of a hotel. My guess is that I would need the GPS on my phone to find my way around inside the place if I lived there.

As I headed toward the front of the house, I saw Bruce, Babbs La-Fleur's personal assistant, come out of the front door and then down the steps of the mansion. I remembered Aunt Anna saying that Bruce was handling the renovation and decorating a wing of the house.

Bruce is the personal assistant to the Queen of Boca Vista, Babbs La-Fleur. Personal assistant by title, but in reality, pretty much Queen Babbs' everything.

Bruce came up to me and gave me a peck on both of my cheeks, and then took me by the shoulders and appraised my looks.

"Well, well, well, you finally took my fashion advice and are looking mighty fine. Makeup not bought at the local drug store," he said as he inspected my eye shadow and lipstick. "Is it Charlie, your new boyfriend?"

I felt my cheeks blush.

"Charlie and I are just friends. We maintain a professional relationship."

"A *professional* relationship, right," Bruce said with his hands on his hips. "Not what I heard from Aunt Anna," he added and winked as he headed for the Corvette.

"Toodles, we'll have to do lunch and catch up, girlfriend, on that *professional* relationship," Bruce said as the roar of the engine took over, and I watched the car disappear down the driveway.

"Aunt Anna," I said as if she could hear me.

My Aunt Anna was always after me to get tips from Jennifer on how I could do better in the romance department since I had not been on the winning team in that department. Recently, though, things were looking up with Charlie, who happens to be Queen Babb's ex. You might even say they were heating up.

I took the steps up the mansion's massive front door and was about to ring the doorbell when the door opened, and there stood Jennifer in all her glory.

Jennifer was, as always, dressed in successful Gold Digger rich, a brand she had recently launched at Wal-Mart, and it was doing very well. Jennifer gave the word bling a new definition. She once told a local reporter that it wasn't cheap to look cheap.

She had a head full of platinum blond and the type of cleavage that could not be store bought, a figure way too petite for the cleavage, and jewelry, lots and lots of jewelry, expensive and flashy. No, there was nothing subtle about Jennifer Stone.

Jennifer handed me a glass of wine and said, "Follow me." As she turned around, I followed her into the mansion. The place was definitely in the midst of a renovation, workers were all over the place, furniture had been moved, and all I could see was scaffolding, paint, drywall and enough tools to supply the local Home Depot.

She moved quickly, and I followed her through the mansion and eventually out to a lanai, which boasted an outdoor fireplace, comfortable seating, a spectacular view of the Atlantic Ocean as far as you could see, and a beach without a soul. Sitting on the table was a bottle of wine. I'm not a wine person, but I knew it wasn't cheap wine.

As her CPA, I was privy to her financial records, both business and personal. Jennifer, although she did her best to hide it, was no dummy.

She had a childlike quality about her and sometimes even a naïveté. She had grown up in poverty in rural Kentucky. She never stopped looking in the rearview mirror. Afraid she would end up where she started, in the hollows of the little town in Kentucky and dirt poor again.

I knew that was not going to happen, but I did see the little girl from Kentucky appear from time to time. That part of her personality was probably what made her so endearing to men and women alike. She was immediately likable.

After a glass of wine and a promise from Jennifer that she would have her chauffeur drive me home, she reached down and pulled out an envelope from a briefcase located next to her chair. As she placed it on the table, Jennifer pointed to it and said,

"MC, I asked you here because I need to talk to you about this envelope." With that, she picked it up and handed it to me.

"Open it."

I took the plain white envelope and looked at it for a second and then looked at Jennifer who had picked up her wine glass and was looking out toward the beach.

I opened the envelope and looked inside. I turned it upside down, shook it, took one last peek, and said, "It's empty."

"Yes, that's why I need to talk to you. You are my financial advisor and a trusted friend. I know you are also a psychic, like your Aunt Sophia."

"Yes, well all those things are true, but what hat am I wearing today, financial advisor, friend, or the DNA I share with my aunts?" I asked placing the envelope back on the table and picking up my glass of wine.

"All three," she said. Interesting, I thought.

"My ex-husband, Harry Stone built this house, and it contains—"

I interrupted and said, "a number of secret rooms. Yes, I remember, is there something more about one of them you want to tell me?"

Jennifer paused here to pick out her words, "Well, let's just say that, during our marriage, Harry used one of them for…storage. After the divorce, I got the house, but he kept one of the secret rooms and had access to that room after the divorce. We had a verbal agreement on that."

Yes, I thought, and I bet that verbal agreement cost plenty in the written divorce agreement.

"The entrances to the secret rooms are well hidden," she said as she filled my glass with more wine. She had shown me the entrance to one of the rooms once. I recalled it was behind some shelves in a large room in her kitchen, which served as a pantry. I nodded my head yes and picked up my glass of wine thinking I might be spending the night at the mansion instead of riding home with the chauffeur tonight.

"So, the mansion came with some strings as part of the divorce," I said, but I already knew the answer.

"He wanted access to that room for storage after the divorce?" I asked.

"Yes, that is precisely it. I guess you could say that room was Harry's storage unit."

"Okay," I said as I sipped a little slower on

the glass of wine, so I wouldn't fall asleep in the chair. Wine had that effect on me.

"Harry gave me that envelope while we were married. He told me if anything happened to him, I was to open it, and I would know what to do. He specifically told me not to open the envelope unless…well, you know."

As she poured another glass of wine and sipped it, out of the blue, I just knew what to ask,

"You didn't wait, did you? You took a peek at the envelope."

The little girl from Kentucky appeared for a moment and then she was gone.

"Of course, I did, but not until after the divorce was final. I figured all bets were off at that point."

"And…" I said. The wine was relaxing me, and my psychic DNA abilities seemed to be working better as a result.

"I got word two days ago that Harry was found shot and killed in Miami. When I went to get the envelope, it was empty."

"Goodness," I said taking this in and then asking,

"Shot and killed? Oh, Jennifer, I am so sorry."

I knew that even though they divorced, they had remained good friends. I also knew that Harry Stone had made his money on Wall Street as a hedge fund manager. When Jennifer had been a new client, she confided in me that she suspected he had ties to questionable groups, maybe even the mafia. So, the manner of his death did not come as a big surprise to me or probably to Jennifer either.

I watched as Jennifer stood and took a few steps forward and looked out over the Atlantic Ocean. She raised her wine glass in a silent toast, and then returned to her seat while brushing away a tear. I sat there for a moment, and then looked down at the empty envelope and asked,

"Jennifer, what was in the envelope?"

"This," she said as she removed a piece of paper from her bra and handed it to me.

"I made a copy of it when I first took a peek in the envelope."

It was folded in half, so I unfolded it. The top half looked like a crossword puzzle, and the bottom half resembled something that looked like the Mona Lisa.

"What is this?" I said as I continued to look at it. The Mona Lisa looked like it had been rubber stamped on the paper. The kind of rubber stamp they use for places where you pay a cover charge.

"This looks like a grid, some kind of crossword puzzle or matrix and below it something that looks like the Mona Lisa," I said, waving it in the air.

"I know. That's why I need your help." I looked at Jennifer, whose face had drawn a blank, and my DNA told me she knew a little bit more than she was telling. That was the way of Jennifer Stone. She dispensed bits and pieces of information on a need to know basis.

"But you said Harry told you if something happened to him to open the envelope and you would know what to do."

"Yes, there was another piece of paper with instructions on who to deliver this paper to. I didn't copy that piece of paper," Jennifer said.

"Why not?" I asked her.

"I didn't have to," she said looking down at a huge rock on her finger.

"You didn't have to because?" Drip, drip, drip, slowly the information was dispensed like an IV.

"That is part of the reason why you are here today. It was Charlie."

"Charlie La-Fleur?"

"Yes."

I just looked at Jennifer and then stared at the puzzle she had just handed to me.

"Charlie," I said with a big sigh. "Great, why am I not surprised?"

"I met Charlie when I married Harry. He was Harry's CPA, and after we divorced, he stayed on as my CPA until I met you. That's all I can think of as to why Charlie's name was on that piece of paper," she said as she pointed a well-manicured finger toward the puzzle I held.

"MC, I need you to bring this to Charlie. That is what Harry asked me to do. I need to honor his request, so I'm asking for your help."

I sat there, but I felt something wasn't quite right. My psychic radar was kicking in.

"Why me? Why not you?"

"You and Charlie are *friends* now," Jennifer said with a wink of her eye.

"Yes, but even so, you could have just as easily made the call."

"I can't."

"Why?" This was now beginning to feel like pulling teeth.

"The detective with the Miami police who called to tell me that Harry had been killed told me it looked like a professional hit," she said.

"When he called he also wanted to ask me some questions about Harry. He told me Harry had been found in his apartment and it had been ransacked. It looked like whoever killed him was looking for something. There wasn't much I could tell him since we've been divorced for several years now, and besides, Harry never shared business details with me. I have decided to beef up my security, though. I also added a security team to have real-time surveillance on my home."

"You did? Why?" I asked, sensing some real concern on her part.

"Aunt Sophia."

"Aunt Sophia suggested you beef up your security detail?"

"No, but I asked her to read the cards, and a King of Spades appeared along with a Jack of Clubs, and a Jack of Spades. She said I should be careful."

What I recall from the many times my mother

and aunts had attempted to teach me how to read the family fortune-telling cards was that these three cards appearing together could be read as a warning to watch your back.

"I'm glad I did," Jennifer said.

"You are?"

"My team found a bug in the house."

"A bug, really?"

"Yes, really."

"They had to call in a special exterminator."

"Oh?"

"Why was that?" Drip, drip, drip, I thought.

"It was something they had not seen before. He told me that it was military grade. Something governments use."

"You're kidding," I said.

"No, the special exterminator told me that it was old school. Nothing current, so it could have been bought by anyone on the black market in the deep web."

"The *deep* web?"

"Yes, the special exterminator told me it's part of the internet that it is well hidden from your average user. He said most people shouldn't go swimming in those waters unless they're looking for trouble."

"Interesting," I said wondering if Sister Matilda was up on that topic.

"MC, I need your help to deliver this to Charlie. You and Charlie see each other so no one would suspect you. Please help me with this. I have to see this through for Harry. It was his wish."

"Do you think this envelope had something to do with Harry's murder?"

I asked knowing the question was coming from the deep dark web of my brain, the psychic part.

"I don't know. Like I said, Harry never discussed his business with me. A bug in the house and the envelope being empty makes me suspicious and more than a little nervous."

"Jennifer, how long has it been since you checked on the envelope?"

"After the divorce, I opened the envelope, and that's when I made the copy. Then I forgot about it. It was kept in one of the secret rooms. After the detective had called me to tell me that Harry had been killed, I checked the room it was kept in again and took another peek. It was there then, and that was about a week ago."

"So you think someone was watching you?"

Jennifer shrugged her shoulders, "It's possible. I've got a lot of workers in the house with the renovation.

"I went to get it today and found the envelope empty. That's when I texted you and asked you to come over."

On my way home, I sat in the back of the chauffeured limousine, pulled out the paper, and sat there staring at it. Was this some sort of code, I thought as I stared at the matrix of mumble-jumble words?

And the caricature that looked like the Mona

Lisa. What did that mean?

The original being gone meant that someone had removed it from the secret room. But, how did they know about the room? How did they get into the house and then into a hidden room? Since it was taken between the time she heard Harry was shot and today, the access window was pretty small. It could have been any number of the people who had been in and out of her house during the renovation. I asked Jennifer if she had any idea how many workers or people had been in her house during that window of time, and she said she thought it had to be at least 30.

"What about the security cameras?" I asked.

"I'll have the security team pull up the video for the brief window of time when the envelope disappeared, but they were only installed outside, not the inside," she told me.

I had also asked, "Does your security team know about the secret rooms? Did you tell them how to access the room where the envelope was kept?"

"No, I decided to keep that information to

myself, but the secret rooms are not locked. They are only hidden from view. You not only have to know where they are but also how to access them."

When I had asked her if she could think of anyone else who could have slipped into the room where she kept the envelope. She just gave me a blank stare, shrugged her shoulders, and said, "It's a big house."

I felt like something weird was going on in my brain. It seemed as if I had seen this piece of paper before. I just didn't know where or when. It felt like a vague memory, but what was really weird was the feeling that Charlie was part of that memory.

Anyway, the talk with Charlie would have to wait since he was out of town for the week. I said good night to Jennifer's chauffeur and headed up to my condo. As I walked to my building, I looked over at the building next door and could see a light still on in my aunt's condo. I almost went up for a visit, but I was beat so I decided to hit the sack. I had placed the puzzle back into its empty envelope and stuck in under my pillow. Still thinking about my afternoon with Jennifer, I dozed off and slept like a baby.

4

The next morning, I arrived at my office and could smell Cuban coffee as I walked in. Velma was not at her command station. I found her in the hallway that was lined with filing cabinets full of records, which a CPA is required to keep. She was fussing with Izzy, her pet iguana. On most days Izzy thinks of himself as human. He basically lives the life of Riley.

He hangs out in my office in his very own beach mansion, which Velma constructed on top of one of the file cabinets. Izzy and I have a love-hate relationship. After all, this is a professional tax and accounting office.

Velma trained Izzy to think he was a small dog. He scratched with his little paws at the front door whenever he wanted to go outside. When Izzy wasn't sunning himself on the docks along the canal, he could be found on his perch, snoozing, and lately snoring. He might have picked up some traits from Velma, like a smart-ass attitude. To keep Velma happy, I, and apparently Rodeo, put up with Izzy. If that wasn't bad enough, my female clients adore Izzy. I have, as of late, found that I was growing fond of him, well almost.

My first client of the day, Gabby, had arrived, and I could hear Velma offering her coffee and chatting. That gave me a few minutes to look over her file and do some quick online tax research.

Gabby was a talker, so her name suited her well. She was eighty-five and recently widowed, and like many of my other clients, very wealthy. She had inherited her wealth at a young age, and I knew she would have questions. Her husband was no longer around to take care of the paperwork, as she called it when we set up the appointment to file her tax return.

Right before I went up to get Gabby for her appointment, I reached into my bag and pulled out the envelope that contained the puzzle and the Mona Lisa. My eyes focused on the Mona Lisa for a moment, and as I did so, I blinked because what looked like a word appeared in the center of the Mona Lisa.

It was like one of those prints where if you stare at it long enough, or move back from it, you see another picture, a picture within a picture, an optical illusion. I could now make out a word, *Money*.

I blinked my eyes and continued to stare at it and moved the paper a little further back and the word *Buried* appeared right above *Money*.

Then my phone buzzed, and I almost jumped out of my chair. I knew it was Velma, and it was time to go up front and get Gabby. I quickly put the puzzle back in the envelope, stuck it in my bag, and got up to fetch Gabby. My mind would not settle down. All during the appointment with Gabby, I kept looking down at my bag anxious to take another peek. At one point when Gabby made a call to one of her kids to ask a question, I pulled out the envelope and puzzle, and sure enough, there were the two words, which my mind now clearly read as *Buried Money*. I stared at it as long as I could, but no other words appeared.

Gabby's appointment ran over, and before long, I had settled into a rhythm. One appointment after another. Each client repeating one of two questions, "How much do I owe?" or "How much will I get back?"

I enjoyed staying busy because the day flew by. Before I knew it, six pm had rolled past. I said good-bye to my last client around seven pm and made sure the front door to my office was locked. Velma had left earlier to pick up her daughters to drive them to a tennis lesson with a well-known coach at Holiday Park in Fort Lauderdale.

Finally, alone, I sat back down at my desk, pulled out the puzzle, and placed it on my desk. I stared at the Mona Lisa until the words *Buried Money* appeared. As I sat there in a daze, Izzy appeared and sat down on the floor behind the chairs facing my desk.

"Geez, don't scare me like that, Izzy."

I got up and made sure he had water in his tiny iguana bowl and iguana food to eat. He ate only organic. I also checked his kitty litter box, and it was clean. I drew the line at emptying his litter box.

Izzy was now standing on his little iguana feet and staring at me or was it something near me?

"He can see dead people" I kept hearing in my head. So I asked Izzy,

"Izzy, can you see someone?" and then out of the blue, "Is it Harry?"

Izzy didn't move, but I looked down at the puzzle on my desk, and it appeared to move ever so slightly. At least my mind thought it did. As if a gentle breeze had swept through the room, but no window or door was open. I had never met Harry, so it wasn't like I could strike up a conversation with him. As I sat there, I felt a chill in the room, and a cold shiver moved up and down my spine. For some reason, I felt very calm.

I looked down at the puzzle again and said to the coolness in my office while staring at Izzy, "I see the words *Buried Money*, which sounds like buried treasure to me." I guess I would have jumped through the ceiling if I heard a voice say "correct." Although I felt like that was exactly what my mind heard.

"Okay. Directions for Jennifer were to contact Charlie." And then from the psychic side of my brain, I added, "In the event of your death. I'm sorry, but I understand you are dead."

"Yep," my mind heard from the chill in the room.

"Well, Charlie is out on a fishing trip. No surprise there, right? As soon as he gets back, I will talk to Charlie about this paper you left for Jennifer to give to Charlie. Once again, I am sorry you are no longer with us."

"Thank you," my mind heard, and then I asked,

"So, did your death have something to do with this piece of paper?" I pointed to the puzzle. As I sat there, a breeze came along out of nowhere and blew the paper right off my desk.

Then the room suddenly thawed out.

"Wow," I said out loud. I picked up the paper

and brought it back to my desk.

I looked at Izzy who yawned at me, and then hopped up on his perch, settled in, and got ready for a good night's sleep.

I walked over to my office bar, poured a shot of cream sherry, trying to cut back on the shots of ouzo. I sat back down and picked the paper up again. I looked at it for a long while, but no new words appeared. I sat there for a long time trying desperately to come up with a rational explanation for what had just happened.

So, I put it on the shelf in my brain, that place where I put all my no-reasonable-explanation-for-this-one items. The shelf was crowded, but it allowed me to let it go, like making a list. All those items on that list numbered and placed in an orderly fashion on a clean piece of paper, instead of floating around the brain, bumping into each other.

I was getting ready to stick the puzzle paper back into my bag when my eye caught something shining on the floor. I walked over and picked it up. It was a gold doubloon.

"What the heck?" I said, and just then my cell rang. It was Charlie.

"Charlie, where are you?"

"Out at sea my, lovely, but I thought I'd give you a call while I was near a cell tower and let you know I was heading home and should be back tomorrow evening. How about if we meet for drinks at Hotel Florida and see where the evening takes us? Ernie is working then, and we both know he makes a mean margarita."

I could almost see the wink in his eye when he mentioned the mean margarita. He was hinting at a night a very long time ago when we were both between spouses, and several mean margaritas resulted in the removal of our clothes later that evening. Jose Cuervo, always a friend of mine.

Ernie was a longtime acquaintance having worked with him on joint task forces while at the IRS. The government agency he worked for would join forces with the IRS to track down a bad guy.

My job was to find a paper trail through

financial records. Once I found it, Ernie's job was to track down bad guys using the paper trail.

Allegedly he was semi-retired and worked part time as a bartender at a tiki bar on A1A known as Hotel Florida. From time to time he was called out of retirement. Like Velma's Rodeo, he usually told everyone he had worked for Homeland Security, probably not who he actually worked for, but it was a good enough alibi. His response to any specific questions was usually "I would tell you, MC, but then I'd have to kill you," and by the way he said it, I knew he wasn't joking.

Before I could say anything, I heard Charlie fading out of signal range.

"Got to go, see you tomorrow about happy hour."

I sat back down with my piece of gold. Many times, I have found coins and have been told that the coins are a message from a loved one who has crossed over.

As I sat there wondering where the heck this piece of gold came from and what it could possibly mean, I looked at the puzzle again feeling like the psychic part of my brain was trying to tell me something, and then I saw it.

I looked again at the block of mumble-jumble words right above the Mona Lisa, a crossword puzzle that didn't spell out anything coherent. I then noticed a series of numbers embedded in the puzzle. They were the only numbers on the mystery paper. At the end of one line were the numbers 245551, and at the end of the next line were the numbers 817800.

I recognized the numbers. Charlie had decided to teach me a little about navigation the last time we were out on his boat. The numbers were the latitude and longitude coordinates for Key West, the city built on the southernmost tip of the United States. I remembered our conversation. Charlie had told me that a bar sits pretty close to the tip of what he called the tailbone of the U.S. The reason I remember the numbers as the coordinates of Key West is because those same numbers just happen to be on a T-shirt he wears from a Key West bar.

Charlie was wearing it the last time we were together. I now connected the dots. I got on my computer and pulled up bars in Key West; and there it was, the name of the bar on his T-shirt, Buried Money. I sat there a little while longer and then stuck the gold coin in the envelope. No longer empty, the envelope was filling up.

5

I got up the next day and went for a run and then back to my condo to get ready for the day. I live in the same condominium complex as my Aunt Sophia and Aunt Anna, along with a good number of others getting up there in age. I used most of my buyout from Uncle Sam when my job with the IRS was abolished to open my tax office and made use of the rest to buy a small condo close to my mother and my aunts. My mother found it, and I remember when she told me about it, she explained to me that it was a deal and was going fast since it was a "fast deal."

It was actually a short sale. She had a habit of shuffling words having learned English as a second language to Greek. She was right, it was a deal. In the end, I bought it, and she reminded me often that she would have never found it if it wasn't for her habit of regularly bribing Saint Anthony.

My cell rang as I was hopping into my car.

"Hello."

"MC, it's me, Charlie. I am stuck in Key West for another day with engine issues. I'll call you when I have an idea of how long the repairs will take. Hold that margarita for me," he said, and then the signal dropped.

Dang, I thought. I was very anxious to talk to him about Jennifer's puzzle paper and turn the mystery over to him, but it would have to wait another day. I had to admit I also was a little disappointed because I was also looking forward to seeing Charlie and having those mean margaritas. "Hold that thought," I said out loud while making my way through slow traffic to the office.

I had first met Charlie while working at the IRS. He was also a CPA at the IRS and later went out on his own. Charlie had a genius IQ and was part wheeler-dealer, part con man, and to top it off, he was a real charmer. A southern gentleman with a drawl and politeness about him that could charm the paint off the side of a barn.

I parked and was heading toward my office when I saw Velma waiting outside next to a parked limousine. As soon as she spotted me, she started walking toward me.

"You might want to get back in that car and come back in an hour or two."

"I would like to, but as I recall I have appointments later this morning with deadlines to file. What's up?"

"Red Hat is waiting for you."

"You mean Bishop Michael?"

"Yep, he said it would only take a few minutes, but he needed to talk to you about the audit."

"Oh, great, well might as well head in and see what he has to say."

"He's not alone. He brought his boss with him, and they didn't arrive by Greyhound bus," she said nodding her head toward the limo.

"His boss?" I said.

"Yeah, and he *is* wearing a Red Hat. The cardinal, the one Sister Hildegard told us about, Cardinal Peter Sole."

Good grief. Talk about an ambush! I followed Velma back into my office to find Bishop Michael and a Red Hat waiting for me. You would never guess one was a Catholic bishop and the other a cardinal.

Both were dressed in suits, and from the looks, probably expensive. Bishop Michael looked trim and had a golfer's tan, which he didn't acquire from the inside of a church. The cardinal wore the red beanie; he was older, gray hair cropped short, almost military style, and tall, like Sister Hildegard. They both got up, and without even a hello Bishop Michael said,

"We need to talk about your handling this matter for the Sisters of Saint Anthony."

"I would be happy to discuss it, but I have a full day of appointments with my clients, and they will start arriving very soon."

"We apologize, but this will only take a minute of your time, Ms. Mahoney," the man wearing the Red Hat said with a polite smile.

"All right," I said.

I led them into my office where they sat down across from my desk. I watched as the bishop got up and faced Velma at the door and then proceeded to close the door in her face. *He'll regret that.* Then I watched him make his way back to the very chair Sister Hildegard had occupied just a few days earlier.

"Ms. Mahoney, this is Cardinal Sole. He is on his way to New York and then back to Rome. He happened to be in the neighborhood," Bishop Michael said.

"Nice to meet you, Cardinal Sole," I said. Never having met a cardinal I wasn't sure how to address him, but I knew Red Hat was out of the question.

"Your Eminence," Bishop Michael said with a smirk as if he could read my mind.

"No need for formality," Cardinal Sole now spoke again with his polite smile.

"Thank you," I said.

For something urgent, they were now quiet, so I got right to the point.

"So, you want to talk about the audit?"

"It's not an audit," Bishop Michael said. "It's called a visitation. I'm not sure what Sister Hildegard has told you, so I can only guess. To get to the bottom line, there is no need for your involvement in this matter. It's a private matter between the church and the Sisters of Saint Anthony. We are here today, as a courtesy, to make it clear to you that this matter is between the Vatican and the Sisters of Saint Anthony—only. To put it in simple terms—for you, they are out of line."

I sat there looking at the both of them, all puffed up with their power. The cardinal with his red beanie and solid gold cross around his neck, smiling like a politician and Bishop Michael looking like he was running late for lunch at some swanky country club. So smug were they in their world where the only place a female could hold was one of subservience. The condescending tone used during this conversation had spoken volumes to me. I was not amused.

The bishop continued while the cardinal sat next to him staring directly at me with a look of authority planted on his face. "Sister Hildegard has overstepped her authority, again, and it is time she was reminded of her place."

I had heard enough, and what I said next even surprised me.

"Her place? Are you talking about the place that women in general hold in the church?" I said calmly. I felt like I was back at the IRS meeting with some puffed-up, high-powered attorneys instead of high-powered leaders of the Catholic Church. It made no difference to me.

The cardinal now was looking at me and just when it looked as if he was about to lose his temper the smile reappeared.

"Ms. Mahoney, there will be no need for your involvement in this matter," Cardinal Sole said.

"It involves matters, to be frank, that you do not have the background for understanding."

Oh boy, I thought, the Red Hat is talking to me like I was a school girl and basically saying I'm stupid.

"Cardinal Sole, the Sisters have asked for my help. I gather you both know how persuasive they can be, or you would not have shown up on my doorstep, unannounced, so early this morning. I have already told them I would help them out with the *audit*," I said calmly.

"No, you will not help them out with the *audit*," Bishop Michael said.

It was beginning to sound like good cop, bad cop.

"Well, then we will have to agree to disagree," I said wondering what this was really about. Why were a Catholic bishop and cardinal sitting in my office at the crack of dawn telling me to back off a matter dealing with a group of nuns?

"Your involvement is not needed, and in fact, Ms. Mahoney, it would be detrimental to the cause of the good Sisters of Saint Anthony," the cardinal now said.

"What exactly do you mean?" I asked since that sounded like a vague threat.

"This is a serious matter with wide-ranging ramifications. Catholic nuns in the United States have gone off track, doing things in their own way, and the time to address this is long overdue. This matter is one that, if not corrected, could lead to taking the unfortunate step of recommending to the Pope that he dissolve any religious order of nuns that does not comply with the outcome of their visitation, or as you call it, audit. This would include the Order of the Sisters of Saint Anthony," Cardinal Sole said.

"What? Are you saying that a group of feisty nuns following a less traditional road, but do so from a good and holy place, are going to be kicked out of the Catholic Church?"

"That is an overly dramatic way to put it, but yes. And that also includes anyone who aids them," the Red Hat said. I sat there almost waiting for both of them to say "boo."

"That would be me?"

"Correct," said the Red Hat with the smile back on his face.

"What is really going on here?" I said as Velma stuck her head in and walked up to my desk. She looked directly at the bishop and announced my first appointment had arrived.

"We have taken up enough of your time," Red Hat said as the two of them stood and made their way out of my office. The cardinal turned to speak to me as I followed them. I watched Bishop Michael walk out the front door of my office and get into his waiting limo.

"You need to drop this matter," the cardinal said, absent the smile. "You are a business woman. Think of it this way. If an order of religious nuns is dissolved by the Vatican, it's like a business that loses its franchise. The business eventually dries up, and the owners go broke. Let *us* handle this *audit*," the cardinal said pointing his finger at me for emphasis as he turned and walked right out the front door of my office. I smiled.

Velma and I both shook our heads as I greeted my first appointment of the day waiting patiently with a look of confusion on her face.

"He's upset about an audit," Velma said.

Around lunchtime, I broke to eat a sandwich, and Velma told me that Sister Hildegard had called to say that Sister Clarissa was coming by tomorrow afternoon to conduct the audit.

Velma told me that she had already rescheduled my appointments and told Sister Hildegard that we would be there for the meeting. I quickly brought her up to speed on the meeting with the bishop and the cardinal.

"Velma, we need to get there a little early, so I can have a chat with Sister Hildegard. I need to find out what she has done to ruffle the feathers of a cardinal and a bishop, so much so that they felt they both had to come all the way down to my office to have a face to face chat with me," I said.

"I still can't get over what Cardinal Sole said. That my involvement would be detrimental to the sisters. He implied it could lead to a recommendation to dissolve their religious order. He made it sound like donations would dry up as a result, and they could find themselves out on the street. It was an out and out threat."

"That is so weird," Velma said. "He obviously does not want you to get involved in this audit. Sounds like the Catholic Church wants to keep it behind church doors."

"You are right. You know I should also talk to Aunt Sophia."

The afternoon went by quickly with more interviews of clients and working on their tax returns. It was getting close to the filing date, so I was meeting with procrastinators and filing extensions.

At this point in tax season, I was up to my elbows in alligators. Thank goodness most of the heavy lifting of paperwork can be done on the computer. I wasn't surprised when Velma popped into my office to tell me my last appointment of the day had canceled, again.

"Since my appointment canceled, I'm going to run over to see Aunt Sophia and Aunt

Anna and see what they might know," I told Velma.

My Aunt Sophia and Sister Hildegard had been childhood friends and could have been cut from the same mold. They frequently talked and were close confidants.

"The Sisters actually came up in a conversation with my mother and her church group the other day," Velma said. "They called them saints."

"They did? What did your mother tell you?"

"That they have been pretty busy lately," Velma said. "The word is that the sisters are running an underground railroad at the convent. Women who are victims of domestic abuse, or are pregnant with no place to go, or are just down on their luck sleeping in their cars are being given safe harbor at the convent."

"Wow," I said thinking about what Velma had just told me.

"I am finding it very hard to fathom why something like that would conflict with the strict interpretation of Catholic Church doctrine. So much so that the cardinal would recommend the extreme route of dissolving the order? It just doesn't make sense to me."

I picked up the phone to call Aunt Sophia. She answered and told me they were on their way down to the public access studio and invited me down. I declined the invite. But while I had her on the phone and Velma was hovering over me, I decided to ask her about the activity at the convent.

"Aunt Sophia, this morning I arrived at my office to find a cardinal and a bishop of the Catholic Church waiting for me."

"Good grief," she said. "I didn't know they made house calls. What did they want?"

"They wanted to have a chat with me. And they also told me to keep my nose out of a matter involving Sister Hildegard and the Sisters of Saint Anthony."

"I heard. Sister Hildegard brought up the visitation matter, and, MC, I suggested they speak with you," Aunt Sophia said. "Let's just say it was in the cards."

Of course, it was. I let out a big sigh.

"So, what else did Sister Hildegard say? Aunt Sophia, is there anything else going on? Velma just told me that the latest project Sister Hildegard is running is a women's shelter at the convent?"

Aunt Sophia was silent, and then I heard a deep sigh when she replied,

"I don't know, MC, but what I do know is that the Sisters of Saint Anthony do charitable work for those who show up at their door. They get absolutely no support from the church. They do everything on their own. They've been keeping it quiet, until recently."

"What do you mean, *until recently*?"

"Well, I finally convinced Sister Hildegard to go public with their good works. She finally agreed to do an interview on Montage. We taped it just about the time this whole audit nonsense started."

Montage was my mother's public access show, which my Aunt Sophia took over after my mother died. It's like *America's Got Talent* and *60 Minutes* rolled into one, something that could only happen on public access television. *Maybe that was it.* I remembered what Velma had said, "The bishop and cardinal wanted to keep this matter behind church doors."

I finished my call with Aunt Sophia, and I looked at Velma.

"What?" Velma asked.

"Oh, nothing, other than Sister Hildegard sat down with Aunt Sophia on public access TV and recorded an interview. Sister Hildegard might be going public about a lot of what you just mentioned. Aunt Sophia is just waiting for the green light from Sister Hildegard to air it."

"Wow, good for her. No wonder Red Hat and Red Hat wannabe are so nervous," Velma said as she went up front to check on who had just come in the front door.

It turned out to be a walk-in who kept me busy for the next couple of hours going over a letter he had just received from the IRS asking why he had not filed his tax returns for the last couple of years. Procrastinators. You got to love them unless you're behind them in the express line at the grocery store.

6

When it came to the church and my upbringing as a Catholic, I can tell you I have evolved into what Bishop Michael would call a C&E Catholic, that is I attend church on Christmas, Easter, and a few Sundays sprinkled in between.

When I did attend mass, I sat hoping the priest's sermon would make sense to me, something I could apply to my day to day life. I am still waiting, and I'm not alone. Usually, when the priest is speaking to those in attendance, I glance around and see the same blank stare on many faces and some even taking a nap.

So far, it hadn't materialized. I'd be at church every Sunday if I could listen to someone who spoke to me. I always got up and left around communion time because, in the eyes of the church, I was a sinner for not attending mass every Sunday and because I was divorced. Yep, I was going to hell if I died anytime soon unless I somehow got my marriage annulled.

I looked up how to do it once, but it looked more confusing than the Internal Revenue Tax Code. It's my understanding that to get a marriage annulled you have to show that your marriage was not consummated, or in plain English, there was no sex involved. Really folks? That was not going to happen.

The male dominated hierarchy, which oversees the day to day workings of the Catholic Church, holds tight to its power and hides behind what it calls ancient church doctrine. Nuns in the Catholic Church, like Sister Hildegard and Sister Matilda, who devote their entire life to doing good, are way down the ladder. In fact, in the Catholic Church, women, in general, are second class citizens.

The morning went by quickly in my office. I met with clients and cranked out more tax returns. I looked up, and it was time for lunch and Velma popped in with two Greek salads.

"We need to get over to the convent early and speak to Sister Hildegard before we meet this Sister Clarissa," I reminded her between bites of salad.

"Don't eat and talk," Velma said like a good mother, so we were quiet for a few minutes while the Greek salad disappeared before our eyes.

"Let's go," Velma said as soon as we disposed of the salad containers. We got ready to head out the front door of my office.

Velma made sure Izzy had water and food. We also made sure the air conditioning was always on.

"Stay put," she said as she closed and locked the front door.

No worry there. Izzy would spend the day on his perch, and if he got bored, he would hop up on the ledge that overlooked the canal out back. He had been known to sit there for hours staring out at the water, and the large yachts docked there.

Velma liked to drive, so we hopped into her car and made our way over to the convent. Before long it came into sight. From a distance, it still looked like an old Florida estate. We could see the long-standing main house of the estate close to the front of the property.

"That's where the sisters are housing the women who need a place to stay," Velma said pointing to the old mansion.

My eyes followed the driveway higher up a hill to the convent. The convent had been built in the same architectural design as the main house. It had a Palm Beach feel to it, Mediterranean style barrel tile roof, white stone, tile, and stucco. The convent sat on about ten acres of land surrounded by a wall made out of lava rocks.

"All made possible by the generosity of kind benefactors," I recalled Sister Hildegard telling me while thinking those donations could dry up if the cardinal made good on his threat to disband the order.

We got out of the car and headed to the front door of the convent where we were greeted by Sister Hildegard and Sister Matilda.

"Let's go, Sister Clarissa is already here and is waiting for us in the bomb shelter," Sister Hildegard said as we followed her.

So much for a quick chat before the meeting.

The convent does not actually have a bomb shelter but does have a room in the old mansion that comes close to what could be a bomb shelter in Florida.

The convent sits on land donated to the Sisters of Saint Anthony a long time ago by a wealthy donor. "He was a pirate," Sister Matilda told us during a history lesson about the convent. The donation included the mansion, which was his home during his lifetime.

This old Florida mansion was recently occupied by a clan of gypsies who have since moved on. Velma and I came to know the queen of that clan of gypsies, Bertha, on a matter involving a hunt for a lost jewel. Velma and I were familiar with the room because we had a few meetings with Queen Bertha in it. The room spooked Velma out.

She also hated spiders and, invariably, before she would have a seat at the large ornate table that occupied the room, she would grab a flashlight and check everywhere for spiders.

"If you don't mind, I'll do a double check," Velma said to the look Sister Hildegard always gave her when she brought up the topic. I think Velma also checked for hidden treasure while she was at it.

We all headed into the old mansion and down the narrow stairs to the bomb shelter. Sitting at the head of the table with her back to us was Sister Clarissa. I was expecting another older nun in a habit, but she was not wearing a habit, and from the back, I saw she was dressed smartly in a dark suit. She had blond hair, and it was pulled back in a tight French twist.

Velma wasted no time grabbing a flashlight. She went around the table checking under all the chairs for spiders and other bugs. I watched as she made her way around to where Sister Clarissa was sitting. Sister Clarissa did not budge but instead looked directly at Velma. They locked stares for a few seconds, and Velma returned the flashlight to a large credenza that sat opposite the table.

"Suit yourself." To date, Velma had never met a nun she was afraid of.

"How long has this credenza been here?" Velma asked.

"It's been here since the house and property were given to the order. We have tried to move it, but it's impossible," Sister Matilda said.

"Hmm, wonder if there is anything behind it," Velma said to no one in the room like an echo of my own thoughts.

Sister Hildegard led Velma and me to one side of the large table, and she and Sister Matilda walked over to the other side. The four of us were flanking Sister Clarissa who rose to greet us as Sister Hildegard made the introductions.

Sister Clarissa was as tall as Sister Hildegard and appeared to be in her early forties. Her striking looks were more like a model than a nun. Standing to greet me I could see that her suit was smartly tailored and she was wearing an expensive pair of black stilettos. When she reached out and grabbed my hand, I felt a solid grip anchored by an expensive gold watch. No vow of poverty for this nun. She also looked like she was in great shape, CrossFit shape, actually. She sat, and we all took our spots around the table. Sister Clarissa had strategically placed herself at the head of the table.

"I am here to conduct the visitation for the Order of Saint Anthony," she began in a clear, concise, and firm voice. She reached down and retrieved a pretty thick file folder from a fancy leather briefcase. "Miss Mahoney," she said.

"Call me MC," I responded, might as well try to get comfortable with this woman.

"All right, MC, you and your assistant, Miss—"

"You can call me Velma," Velma said before she could finish her sentence. Once again, the two of them had a quick "I dare you" stare down.

"MC and Velma, before we get started I would like to go over some rules," she said. Of course, I thought, out come the rules of engagement.

"You are both here in the role as witnesses for the Order of the Sisters of Saint Anthony. In that role, you both will be permitted to stay in the room, but you will be quiet. Otherwise, I will ask you to leave. Sister Hildegard this is a matter that does not involve taxes or the IRS. So, there is no need for representation by a CPA."

Listening to Sister Clarissa I could see the lawyer in her by the smug way she addressed Velma and I. Intimidation, it was putting me right at home. Once again, I felt like I was back at the IRS and was dealing with a high-powered lawyer from a law firm representing a very wealthy client during an audit. Sister Hildegard was right, this was right up my alley.

I reached down into my briefcase and pulled out a file folder and handed her a general power of attorney.

"I believe this gives me the right to speak on behalf of the Sisters of Saint Anthony."

She picked it up and handed it back to me without even looking at it.

"No, it does not. This is a matter that does not deal with tax law, it deals with canon law. In the Catholic Church, canon law is comprised of the rules and regulations of the church, similar to the rules and regulations of the Internal Revenue Code. I am a lawyer well versed in canon law, and that is why I am here representing the Vatican."

She then handed Sister Hildegard a piece of paper, which Sister Hildegard looked over and then passed to me. I could see that it was written in Italian with a large seal at the bottom. I assumed this was a Vatican seal, two keys crossed with a papal crown in the middle.

Sister Clarissa continued, "You would not expect me to handle an IRS audit any more than I would expect you to handle a matter before the Vatican."

I pushed my power of attorney back over to her.

"Sister Clarissa, I am not here as a CPA. I am here because Sister Hildegard, as the Mother Superior of the order, asked me, along with my assistant Velma, to be here. You probably don't need this power of attorney, but it will serve its purpose, which is to allow you to speak to me directly."

Sister Clarissa responded stiffly, "That won't be necessary because I will not be speaking to you directly or indirectly on behalf of the Sisters of Saint Anthony. If you wish to remain in the room, you will be quiet."

Sister Hildegard now spoke, "I would have liked to suggest that we begin this audit today. But, since it looks as if we're at a stalemate, Sister Clarissa, to be clear, I *will* ask for MC's assistance when needed. I asked her to be here because she is a trained negotiator, one who can look at an argument from both sides of the fence and resolve a disagreement. But, let's cross that bridge when we come to it."

Sister Clarissa sat there for what seemed to be a long time, then picked up her briefcase and placed the large file back into it, closed it firmly, and rose to leave.

"Sister Hildegard, this is the reason why you and your order are under an *audit*, as you are calling it, by the Vatican. You insist on doing things your way and not the way required by the church. I have no choice but to report this situation back to the bishop and the cardinal. I will also report that our meeting failed to move forward because you insisted on operating by your own rules. Don't bother to rise. I will show myself out."

We watched as Sister Clarissa turned on her stiletto heels and made her way up the stairs. Shortly afterward, we could hear a door shut.

"Well, that went well," I said tongue in cheek thinking she obviously had a game plan from the start, and it didn't include proceeding with this audit if I was present.

"Yes, it did, MC, actually it went just the way we wanted it to," Sister Hildegard said.

I responded, "By the way, the bishop and Cardinal Sole dropped by my office yesterday to have a face-to-face chat. On the way out, the cardinal made a threat to disband the order if things didn't go his way." I took a few minutes to tell Sister Hildegard and Sister Matilda about their visit.

"Well, I had heard the cardinal was in town, and that that the ultimate penalty could be the kicking our order out of the church," Sister Hildegard said not surprised or moved by the cardinal's threat.

She continued, "The longer we can delay this audit the greater the chances that it will be dropped and our prayers will be answered with a new and more modern pope."

"That could be a long time off," I said.

"It's not a long time off. Let's just say it's in the cards," Sister Hildegard said with a smile.

7

Velma dropped me off back at the office. I checked my messages and was disappointed that I had missed one from Charlie saying he was probably going to be stuck in the Keys a few more days taking care of the engine work. He would call back.

I was looking forward to seeing Charlie and wanted to talk to him about Jennifer's situation, but I also wanted to wait until I could speak to him in person. I wanted to hear what he had to say, and something in my DNA told me he would have something important to say. My last message was from Jennifer who said that Charlie had called and left a message after he had heard that Harry was killed. I picked up my phone and called Jennifer who answered with, "Have you talked to Charlie?"

"No, he is stuck in Key West with engine problems. I am waiting until he gets back to show him the paper you gave me. I guess he heard about Harry and called you. Did you mention the puzzle paper to him?"

"Yes, he called, but only to offer his condolences. No, I didn't bring it up. Listen, MC, I can't talk now, Joe is over here, and we are having another one of *those* arguments. Same talk we have had before about marriage, pregnancy, and becoming a full-time, stay at home mom. Here he comes, I'll wait to hear from you about Charlie," and with that, she hung up.

Joe was the son of Boris and Natasha and ran their biggest honky-tonk, the Full Moon Saloon. Joe was never happier than when Jennifer was with him and singing at the Full Moon.

I hate phone conversations, so I decided not to call my aunts, but to head on over to their condo and see what they were up to since I had not had a chance to chat with them.

I locked up my office and got in my car and headed directly over to see my aunts. I rang the doorbell and then was about to use my key when the door opened, and there stood my Aunt Anna, all 60 inches of her. Aunt Anna looked like a munchkin, short and round. She was my *fun* aunt because she had the unique way of making me feel like a kid again.

"MC, get in here. I need to talk to you while Sophia is out."

I walked into the condo she shared with my Aunt Sophia, and she ushered me into their living room. I sat down while she found some Greek wine, which they always have on hand along with ouzo. While I waited, I got up and walked over to their dining room table and placed my hands on the back of the chair that sat at the head of the table. This was where my mom had sat, and my aunts had left it that way. "In case she visits," my Aunt Anna would say, "no changes." Customs and traditions are an important part of Greek culture along with religion and superstitions.

Aunt Anna saw me at the table, handed me a glass of wine, and motioned me back into the living room. She also carried in a big tray of Greek snacks, hummus and crackers, and one of my favorites, tiropetes. She quickly took a sip of her wine as we sat down.

"I brought hummus since it's healthy," my aunt said as she munched on the buttery and flaky phyllo and motioned me with her head to start eating. I joined her and dipped mine in the hummus.

"There, now it's healthy," I said as we laughed and enjoyed the wine.

"What are you up to? Are you in trouble with your older sister?" I asked.

"Heck no, her birthday, which is also her name day is coming up, and I'm planning a surprise party down at the public access studio. I wanted to make sure you could be there, so I am giving you a heads up."

Most Greeks owe their names to a religious saint. In Greece, name days are as important as birthdays. It's really just another excuse for a celebration along with food and more food.

"Of course, I'll be there," I said as we both heard the door open.

I whispered, "What's the date for the party?"

"On her birthday, of course. I'll call you to remind you," Aunt Anna whispered back just as Aunt Sophia came into range.

"MC, so good to see you," Aunt Sophia said as I got up and gave her a big hug.

"What's going on in here, Anna? Why are you whispering?"

"Nothing," I said to my Aunt Sophia while looking directly at my Aunt Anna who was smiling at her sister.

"Aunt Anna was just pouring some wine and feeding me, of course."

She looked hard at both of us but decided to drop it, which was a relief. She poured herself a glass of wine and sat down, and like most Greek women got right to the point.

"At my age, you don't have time to waste," she once told me.

"Any more on the audit of Sister Hildegard and her flock of feisty nuns? I understand you had a meeting." Yep, right to the point. She probably had already talked to Sister Hildegard but wanted to hear my version of the events.

"It's crazy, Aunt Sophia. The Vatican thinks nuns in the U.S. have overstepped their bounds by taking liberal positions on social issues.

"We met with a Sister Clarissa. She's a nun who is also a lawyer and was sent by the Vatican to run the audit. She looks nothing like a nun, by the way. We didn't get very far because she insisted up front that my role was to sit still and keep quiet. She got up and left when Sister Hildegard told her that wasn't going to happen," I said.

"Sister Hildegard's plan is to delay this whole thing until a new and more reasonable pope is in office. The sisters seemed to think that might happen sooner than later. Something about it being in the cards. Since you were the one who first sent them to me, what is that all about?"

"It was in the cards, MC. Your card was the one that appeared when your Aunt Anna,

Sister Hildegard, and I read the cards the first day she heard about this audit."

"Aunt Sophia, why me?" I thought: nuns, psychics, and gypsies, oh dear!

"Because you are special, MC," Aunt Anna said as she piled more food on my plate and re-filled my glass with more wine.

"So, this Sister Clarissa, she sounds like a formidable woman according to Sister Hildegard," my Aunt Sophia said.

"Sister Hildegard told me all about this Sister Clarissa. Rather fascinating individual. A successful Wall Street lawyer before she became a nun," Aunt Sophia continued while taking a sip of Greek wine.

"I wonder why she became a nun," I said.

"Well, Sister Hildegard said she does have a spiritual side, but she's also very ambitious," Aunt Sophia said.

"So, Aunt Sophia, you taped an interview with Sister Hildegard down at the public access TV studio?" I decided to get to the point like the other women in my family.

"Yes, we did. It's time the world knew about the good work the Sisters of Saint Anthony do for the many causes they have embraced," Aunt Sophia said.

"You betcha," which was my Aunt Anna's usual reply to her older sister's comments.

"The interview will help with more donations, which they could use to carry on these good works," my Aunt Anna said receiving an approving nod from her sister.

"Well, how soon are you planning on airing this interview?"

"I wanted to air it right away, but Sister Hildegard asked me to wait," Aunt Sophia said.

"Yeah, she said she wants to keep it for leverage just in case the bishop causes them big trouble like putting them out on the street," Aunt Anna said and followed up with "ftou, ftou, ftou."

"Anna." My Aunt Sophia now spoke.

"We agreed reluctantly to hold off airing the interview until she gives us the green light.

She felt the time was not right. But, I don't agree. I don't trust the bishop or this Sister Clarissa."

Aunt Sophia left the room for a moment and then returned with a DVD.

"Here is a copy. You should watch it and then keep it in a safe place. It might come in handy while you are conducting this audit."

I spent the rest of the evening visiting with my aunts, drinking Greek wine, and eating Greek food. We laughed and told the usual stories, about my mother who had been a cross between Aunt Sophia, wise and strong, and Aunt Anna, always up to some kind of mischief.

At the end of the evening, my aunts loaded me up with doggie bags and sent me home. Luckily my condo was in the same complex, so it was only a short walk to my building.

Later that night I sat down and watched the DVD. It was very moving to listen to Aunt Sophia interview Sister Hildegard as she explained how they reached out and helped those in very desperate situations. These same nuns, who I had viewed as the nuns from my parochial school hell, worked hard to help people from all walks of life that had fallen on hard times.

I sat quietly after viewing the interview thinking the Sisters of Saint Anthony were a bomb waiting to go off. It was the type of interview that could go viral, kindly nuns doing charitable works and the powerful Catholic Church harassing them. Public opinion would be on the side of the sisters. It would certainly dampen any aspirations the bishop had of becoming the first American pope.

I watched it again and realized that it was as good as any *60 Minutes* interview. You had to love them, a grandmotherly Aunt Sophia interviewing a formidable nun on public access TV. It couldn't get any better than that. I put the DVD away in a safe place. I knew in my heart I would do whatever I could to help these nuns. They were good women following their mission to help souls find their way home. Just like their patron, Saint Anthony.

As I fell asleep, I could hear my mother's voice,

"You need to drop by St. Mary's. Bribe Saint Anthony and light some candles."

Yes, I will do that. Light some candles for my mother and those who had passed before me.

8

Bishop Michael Roosevelt met with his brother, Senator Walther Roosevelt, at a favorite watering hole in Cocoa Beach, *To the Moon Alice*, a bar that had been around since the beginning of the space missions at NASA.

Walther ordered a club soda and then watched his brother order a second martini. He had given up drinking as soon as he became a serious contender for the vice-presidential slot, but unfortunately, his brother, despite his pleadings, had not followed suit. Michael had called and begged to meet. Walther was in Florida for a fundraiser, so he agreed. Michael was dressed as usual as if he had just finished a round of golf because that's exactly what he had done. Probably wise, though, not dressing like clergy in a bar while downing martinis early in the afternoon.

Walther and his younger brother, Michael, had been raised in a traditional Catholic family.

After college, his younger brother followed his lead, both had attended law school and were on a fast track to successful careers. Walther went to work for the Department of Justice where he rose to a prominent position as a U.S. Attorney.

His brother Michael headed to Wall Street directly after his graduation from Harvard Law, but he had a drunken Chappaquiddick style accident that killed the love of his life and two others while he survived with only minor injuries. He went to prison where he had no choice but to sober up and where he found religion. Upon his release, he surprised everyone and joined the Jesuits where he used his inherent ambition and his law degree to advance in the hierarchy of the Catholic Church. He had become a bishop and was not shy about letting it be known that he had his sights on becoming the first American pope. However, his drinking problem had reappeared in spades and was only making his obsession worse.

The senator listened to his brother tell him about nuns going radical and how he and this Cardinal Sole planned to get them in line.

"You need to quit drinking. I can get you help. Why don't you take a break from this Vatican thing and the nuns? Come to Washington. We can do it discreetly."

"I know, you're right, but I can't leave now. Not with this whole visitation thing going on. All these nuns who are way out of line. The Vatican has sent a real sharp lawyer to handle the matter, and even she is having problems handling them. We are starting our first visitation with the Order of the Sisters of Saint Anthony right here in my diocese. Once this is handled and I'm in the clear, I will stop drinking."

"Michael, really, what the heck is this all about? My God, they're nuns. Leave them alone to do their work."

"You don't understand their work. They have gone over-the-top liberal. Their work needs to be pulled back in line with the strict teachings of the Catholic Church," he said leaning over as if he was sharing top secret information. He spilled his drink.

Grabbing the attention of a waiter to clean up the spill, Walther responded, "Come on, Michael, the church is not going to win on this issue. Are they crazy? Catholic people in this country love their nuns. Frankly, if you ask me, the Catholic Church needs to come into the current century with its archaic doctrine and fall in line with these nuns."

"I need your help. You remember MC and Velma?"

Walther stopped for a moment and then gave his brother his undivided attention.

"Like a recurring bad dream. Are they back?"

"Yes, and Sister Hildegard has hired MC to represent them during the visitation or as they are calling it, the *audit*."

Walther sat there for a moment and thought about what his brother was telling him. MC had been a thorn in his side when she was with the IRS, and he had been with the DOJ. He thought he had dealt with her then, but she just kept coming back to spoil his plans. At some point, he knew he may have to deal with her on a more—permanent basis.

"I can't get involved with this now, Michael. You need to handle MC and Velma on your own. Didn't you tell me this Vatican lawyer, Sister Clarissa, was a tough cookie? Use your people, Michael. Get this nun from Rome to handle MC and Velma. If you want my advice, I would say to you if you really want to become the first American pope, drop this audit and take a bold stand on cleaning up the church. Investigate all the scandals your brother bishops have swept under the rug."

Michael quietly listened to his brother. This was the same argument coming from cardinals who leaned toward the liberal side of the church. But, to his mind, strict adherence to conservative doctrine was the path to order. He would talk with Sister Clarissa and instruct her to use whatever tactics were necessary to get MC and Velma either in line or out of the way and Saint Anthony's nuns under control. Even if it led to the closing down of the order that Cardinal Sole was pushing for.

It was his big chance. Cardinal Sole had assured him he would recommend him for a cardinalship once these audits were successfully concluded.

He had to take control of his backyard and get these nuns in line if he had any chance to advance to a position in Rome.

Walther had one of his men drive his brother back to his hotel. Michael went straight to the bar and continued to drink until it was late. He didn't see the man who drove him back to the hotel watching him at the bar or follow him to his room.

"He's in his room now, sir."

"Good, that's all for now. He should be good to return to his residence in the morning with a nasty hangover," Walther said.

He picked up the phone and dialed.

"This is U.S. Senator Roosevelt. I am Bishop Michael's brother, and I would like to speak with Cardinal Sole."

The last thing I need is for my brother and that cardinal of his opening the doors to the convent property. That would be a disaster.

9

The next day before heading to the office, I drove over to the convent under the premise of talking to Sisters Matilda and Hildegard about the audit. Secretly I wanted to pick their brains about Jennifer's puzzle, specifically the psychic part of their brains.

They suggested going for a walk in the convent garden, and Sister Matilda began a history time lesson about Saint Hildegard. It didn't matter that I had heard the story a hundred times before because, with Sister Matilda, history bore repeating. She made it come alive. Sister Hildegard had walked up ahead knowing the story by heart; having chosen the name Hildegard as her religious name when she had become a nun. I looked ahead to where she was checking some plants and pulling a few weeds.

"Saint Hildegard was not only a woman way ahead of her time, but she also had a thorough understanding of herbs and their natural healing powers," Sister Matilda said.

I knew it was Sister Matilda's idea to name the convent's garden after Saint Hildegard. We caught up now with Sister Hildegard who continued pulling weeds and tending to a small group of plants. Sister Hildegard stood and pointed at a row of green plants each with seven to nine leaflets. "This is our herb garden," Sister Hildegard said.

I had been to this part of Saint Hildegard's garden before. It was expanding.

"The convent's gardener, a hippie from way back, is growing these herbs for medicinal purposes. These herbs are only given to those who find them beneficial while undergoing chemotherapy," she said.

"MC, I know this from personal experience, having undergone chemo and radiation. It helped me regain my appetite and gave me the strength to finish the treatments," Sister Hildegard said while bending to pull a few more weeds.

I looked at Sister Hildegard and then took a closer look at the plants. The plants gave off an odd aroma. As I looked closer at the plants and thought about Sister Hildegard, it only confirmed what I had been thinking all along. I knew immediately what they were growing in their garden.

Sister Matilda spoke, "Saint Hildegard of Bingen grew these very plants. These are holy plants. Saint Hildegard was also a mother superior. She was a remarkable woman. To this day she is known for her medicinal use of plants as a natural healer. She also was a mystic."

"I am honored to have taken her name," Sister Hildegard said as Sister Matilda bowed her head and smiled.

"It would certainly be a blessing if one day a cure for cancer was found. Especially if it was something that all along was right in front of our noses," I said.

"You know, one of my clients was telling me the other day that she is concerned about the rising cost of her cancer treatment."

"We are paying too much for prescription drugs," Sister Hildegard said with a distinct tone of anger in her voice.

"Our own sisters cannot afford to pay for their medications."

"The price for cancer drugs can exceed $100,000 a year. Even with health insurance, out-of-pocket costs can run as much as $25,000 a year. That is more than half the typical family's income," Sister Matilda said.

"What can people do?" I asked.

"It's a life or death question."

"Did you know, MC, that one cancer drug that prolongs life by years and another by days are priced the same? A drug on the market that may add three to four months of life to a cancer patient costs $150,000 a year."

"You're kidding?"

"No, I'm not kidding. Why do you think we're growing these herbs? It calmed me down many a night during my treatment. The sad thing is that one-quarter of the cancer patients being treated don't take their medications as prescribed. Some of them due to the cost and some because of the horrible side effects. These herbs help to give them the strength to continue. Of course, Bishop Michael and Cardinal Sole would not understand the type of herbs we grow in our garden, so we must be very cautious," Sister Hildegard said staring at the herb garden.

"Of course," I said.

"It makes an excellent tea and is also good in brownies," Sister Matilda whispered. I just nodded thinking, "What next?" with these two nuns.

The three of them reached a small gazebo and sat down, which gave me some time to think of a way to approach the puzzle.

"So, what's on your mind, MC?" Sister Hildegard asked. So much for a plan to broach the subject sideways. These two were skilled psychics.

I reached down and pulled out the envelope that contained the mysterious sheet of paper and handed it to Sister Hildegard, who looked at it for a moment and then passed it to Sister Matilda, who took a while longer to study it. She then turned it upside down, and sideways, and backward, and then gave it back to me.

"Where did you get that?"

"From a friend, it was given to her by her former husband. It was in an envelope, and she had been given instructions not to open it until after his death. He recently died, rather suddenly. She had been instructed, upon his death, to give this piece of paper to a particular person. She gave it to me to figure out what it meant before it's handed over to that person. As you can see, it's a bit of a puzzle."

"So, you know who that particular person is?" Sister Matilda asked.

"Yes."

They sat there for what seemed to be an eternity, and finally, I had to say,

"Well, do you have any idea what this is all about?" I asked.

Sister Hildegard got up and said, "Follow me."

I got up and followed the two out of the garden and across the property, up a hill in back of the convent, to the cemetery. They walked along the gravesites until they came to a large monument.

"This is the gravesite of the gentleman who was so kind to leave all this property to our order," Sister Hildegard said raising her hands in a circle.

"He was a pirate," Sister Matilda said.

I looked down at the gravestone and read the name out loud, "Grover P. Stone." The dates he lived and died were beneath his name. I also saw more numbers at the bottom of the stone. I looked at my piece of paper and then back at the gravestone.

"They are the same numbers."

"Yes, latitude and longitude for Key West," Sister Matilda said.

"What's his story?" I asked.

"Well, like Sister Matilda said, Mr. Stone was a pirate, mostly in spirit, but the story goes that he was a descendant of the famous pirate, Blackbeard. Sister Matilda figured out the numbers on his gravestone were the coordinates for Key West, but we had not given it much more thought than that. All we knew about him was that he owned a business in Key West before he moved here and built this mansion."

"We heard it was a bar and that it may have been frequented by Hemingway and his gang of friends," Sister Matilda added.

"We suspected he found some of his famous ancestor's treasure because he left Key West and the bar one day. He arrived in Fish Camp and built himself a mansion. Along with this property, he also left a nice donation to the order when he died."

"There have always been rumors of hidden treasure buried on the convent property. But it's not like we were going to start digging to search for buried treasure or take a trip down to some Key West bar to look for treasure," Sister Hildegard said.

"We would stand out as your not-so-typical treasure hunters," Sister Matilda said.

"I'm really baffled now," I said looking at the piece of paper.

"Don't be," Sister Hildegard said.

"You were meant to bring that piece of paper to us, and we can only conclude that it has something to do with this pirate who has been very kind to our order."

"Because the paper shows the same numbers—the latitude and longitude for Key West—that are on his gravestone?" I asked.

Both Sister Matilda and Sister Hildegard looked at each other and then at me as if exchanging some words only they could hear.

"What do you think is the significance of the words 'Buried Money' and 'the Mona Lisa'?" Sister Matilda now asked.

"You can see the words 'Buried Money'?"

"Clear as day," Sister Hildegard said.

"I know Buried Money is the name of a bar in Key West. I still don't know what to make of the Mona Lisa."

"That bar in Key West may well be the same bar Mr. Stone owned. Like I said, we knew he lived in Key West and then picked up and left one day. He also liked to drink," Sister Matilda said. "His middle name was Peter, and he liked to be known by his nickname, Pirate Pete."

"Who is the person that is to be contacted? Someone you know?" Sister Hildegard asked.

"Yes, I said, my friend, Charlie."

"Oh, the one who has a big crush on you," Sister Matilda nearly squealed.

Aunt Anna, I thought, as I looked the other way.

"I didn't teach school for all those years and not be able to recognize that look, MC."

I told them the story of how I came to have the paper. Then they were both staring at me again with that strange look and then somewhere I couldn't see.

"So, your friend Charlie, does he know about this bar in Key West?"

"Yes, as a matter of fact, he's probably there right now having a drink. His boat was having engine problems. The last he said to me was that he was heading there while his boat was being worked on."

"Well, this is a sign. You need to go to Key West and bring this paper to Charlie. He'll know what to do with it. Plus, you can—you know—visit," Sister Hildegard said with a mischievous smile on her face, which was mirrored by Sister Matilda.

"Are you saying this is some kind of sign, that Charlie is at the bar known as Buried Money and I am here at the place where Pirate Pete is buried? I should just drop everything and head down to Key West?"

"Yes, pretty much. Whether you go or not is up to you, of course. Free will, you know," Sister Hildegard said.

"Signs can come to you, whether you are psychic or not has nothing to do with it. Always keep your mind open for something out of the ordinary," Sister Matilda said.

"Like what?"

"Well, spirits use energy to send a message to us, and many times it is with an animal—say, Izzy, for example. Has anything like that happened lately?"

I thought back on Izzy and the feeling of a presence in my office.

"Yes, actually, it has," I said. "And yes, it involved Izzy."

"Well, pay attention. It may happen again. It might be something as simple as a butterfly. Many times, I will see a butterfly land right in front of me, or I will see a ladybug through a window pane. Or I will find a coin while thinking of someone who has passed. These are common signs from those on the other side of the shore," Sister Matilda said.

"Let us know what happens because I have a good feeling our order is part of that puzzle," Sister Hildegard said.

"Because of Pirate Pete?"

"Yes," Sister Matilda said. "And because, if you look very carefully at that Mona Lisa, you will see she is wearing a habit."

I looked down at the paper and at the Mona Lisa. Sure enough, she was wearing what looked like a nun's habit, not unlike the one worn by the nuns of the Order of Saint Anthony. And then my eyes wandered to the gravestone. Gold doubloons were etched into the granite, very much like the one I found in my office.

10

"Can you get away for a couple of days," I asked Velma once I got back to the office.

"Well, not really." she said "But I sure would like to. What do you have in mind?"

"I was just told by our favorite feisty nuns that I've gotten a sign that I need to take a road trip to Key West."

"Really? Hmm, my kind of sign," Velma chuckled.

I took a few minutes and told Velma about the puzzle paper, and my meeting at the convent.

"Geez, let me see that piece of paper."

I got it out and showed it to Velma.

"What do you see?"

"I see what looks like a crossword puzzle and something that looks like that famous painting," Velma said.

"Oh yeah, wait a minute. I see it now, a nun who looks a lot like the Mona Lisa."

"Interesting." *Hmm, maybe Velma sees more than she realizes.*

"Let me call my sister Cassie and see if she can watch the girls for a few days. She should be thrilled to spend time with them being their favorite aunt."

I tried to call Charlie again but got voicemail, again. So, I sent a text telling him we were heading to Key West tomorrow.

I looked up, and Velma was walking back into my office with a big grin on her face.

"Cassie can do it. Road trip! I'm so excited. We'll be like Thelma and Louise," she said and then she headed up front to greet a day full of clients.

The day went by quickly with lots of work accomplished on my client's taxes.

"Yep, Thelma and Louise, I love it. You're coming home with me. My girls can watch you while we're gone," Velma said as she scooped Izzy up to take him home.

"We'll meet back here in the morning," I said as I waved good-bye to Izzy, who seemed to have his happy face on.

My cell rang. It was Charlie.

"Well, I am excited you are heading down here but would have been happier if it was just you alone."

"I know, me too, but this involves some urgent business I have to talk to you about. Something I wanted to talk to you about in person. It involves Jennifer Stone and her ex-husband Harry?"

"Yes, I heard he was killed. That must be hard on Jennifer," he said with a pause on his end.

"I am bringing an envelope that was left for you by Harry. Jennifer wants me to give to you. Harry left instructions to have it delivered to you in the event of his death. Did you know about the envelope?"

"Yes, when I heard about his death, I remembered it. Harry told me about it a long time ago. It should contain some instructions for me."

"Well, I've got it. I'll be bringing it with me."

"Along with Velma. Didn't want to find yourself alone on this boat with me?"

"No, of course not," I said while thinking I didn't trust myself alone with him on his boat or anywhere else.

"Really, MC?" Charlie asked. "Okay, I'll see you tomorrow. We might as well meet at Buried Money. By the way, MC, I need to warn you. I'm pretty sure I saw your ex-husband and his boat pull in the Galleon Marina today."

"What? Are you sure?" I said. *Another freaking sign?*

"It's hard to miss a 75-foot Jacques Cousteau-looking ship set up for underwater research with the name Mary Catherine in large, bold, block letters. Ernie said he might be in Key West, something about working with the Navy."

I hung up and walked over to the office bar and poured myself a shot of ouzo. Great, just what I needed Charlie and my ex-husband, Theo, both in Key West. Yes, this was a freaking sign all right. My two worlds were now colliding, so much for a normal love life.

11

Theo was my ex-husband, and according to my mother, he was also my soul mate. My mother loved Theo, short for Theodoros, as did my two aunts and anyone who came within five feet of him. One just fell under his spell.

I met Theo when I was young and just starting to work at the IRS as an agent. In fact, Charlie was a new agent, too. He and Charlie hit it off. They both had a love of the sea, and I suspect, knew each other in another life, probably they had both been pirates.

From the beginning, I knew there was an attraction between Theo and me. This sparked a friendly competition between Theo and Charlie. Secretly, I was flattered.

After Theo and I married, he left the IRS and went to work as a tax attorney at a high-powered law firm. I had known from the day

I had met him that my Theo had a gypsy soul.
After a while, I could see he was restless.

"He needs to have a good cause to fight for.
It's part of his spirit and always will be," my
mother's words.

Theo and I sat down one night to talk. He told
me he was not happy, he was going to quit
the law firm, and he planned to buy a boat
and head out to sea.

"Really?" I remember saying.

The thought of taking off and leaving my
very comfortable life and job was daunting.
Not to mention my fear of the water.

"Will you come with me?"

I was speechless. The next day we talked
again.

"I know you, MC, and I know you are not
ready, but I am. I will go, and this will give
you time to adjust to the idea. I will be
waiting for you."

So, he did. But as he drifted off to sea so did
our marriage. After a couple of years, we

agreed to divorce, so that I would be free to choose whether or not to join him. He has made it very clear to me that he is still waiting.

I locked up the office and headed home to pack for the trip tomorrow and to get a good night's sleep. Something told me I was going to need it.

12

Saturday morning, I arrived at the office to meet Velma, and she had Izzy with her.

"Sorry, he has to come with us. Cassie was not onboard for babysitting Izzy," she said.

I looked at Izzy, and he looked back at me through the car window with the "I promise to be good" look on his iguana face.

"Yeah, you better," I said to him.

I looked in the back of her SUV, and she had luggage and Izzy's crate and stuff as she called it. I found places for my luggage and gave Izzy another "you better behave look."

Velma spoke up, "He can stay out on the dock next to Charlie's boat. He'll be fine."

"Of course, he can," I said looking at Izzy as I got into the car and could see that he had made himself right at home for the ride.

I knew he wouldn't be spending much time on the dock since Charlie had a fondness for Izzy. He'll probably be on the aft deck. I thought I detected a little iguana smile at the mention of Charlie's name.

We jumped onto I-95 and headed south to Key West.

We traveled through Fort Lauderdale and Miami, and before long we had passed Key Largo and entered the land of pirates. The breezes were those of gypsy souls as my mind wandered to the thought of seeing Theo again in Key West. How appropriate, I thought, since that was where he proposed to me all those years ago.

Fast forward to Charlie and me, and my mind was about to explode.

"Are you okay?" Velma said.

"No," I said.

"Charlie thought he spotted Theo's boat in Key West at the Galleon Marina."

"Dang," she said.

Velma had been my maid of honor at our wedding.

"Well, this should be interesting."

"Was he sure it was his boat?"

"Yep, there aren't many boats there decked out like Theo's with the name Mary Catherine in big, block letters."

"Yep," Velma said. "Be good to see him again." Velma had also been taken by Theo's charm.

We were quiet as Velma drove the road to Key West, sometimes also known as the Overseas Highway. It's a 113-mile highway taking US 1 through the Florida Keys.

It is now a major coastal highway between Miami and Key West. Travelers on this highway enter an exotic world of tropical trees and plants. The American crocodile and Key deer are native to the tropical islands of the Florida Keys.

You can fly from Miami to Key West in 45 minutes, but you would miss a memorable road trip across coral and limestone islands connected by forty-two bridges, one of them known as the Seven Mile Bridge with its 65-foot arch, which permits tall ships to pass beneath it.

Countless honky-tonk towns were surrounded on both sides by intense blue and emerald green water. Deep below laid the wrecks of hundreds of Spanish galleons sunk in the 15th century. The nearly constant ocean breeze often found me at the end of the day marveling at sunsets that made me raise a glass in a toast.

We decided to stop in Marathon, the capital of the middle Keys for lunch. Marathon runs about eight miles along the road to the Keys and holds a population under 10,000. Recently I learned from Charlie that its waters were some of the best in the world for salt water sportfishing. As I thought about Charlie, it struck me that he was not that different from Theo. He would also drop everything to take off and spend his days on a boat. The difference would be that Charlie would be fishing.

We stopped at the Sunset Grill for grouper sandwiches, and I was tempted to stay and hang out at the bar, but Velma pulled me back to the car.

"Let's get going," she said, "we're almost there."

13

By late afternoon, we drove into the historic Old Town district of Key West, and there was a brisk breeze blowing. I was immediately struck by the architecture. It had the largest assortment of wooden frame buildings in Florida.

Key West is the southernmost city in the continental United States with Cuba a scant 94 miles further south. This makes Key West closer to Havana than to Miami. *Cayo Hueso* is the original Spanish name for Key West. It literally means *bone cay*. It is said Key West was once littered with remains (bones) of prior native inhabitants who used the land as a communal graveyard. Key West is also the southernmost point of U.S. 1 and State Road A1A, and right about that spot sits the bar, Buried Money.

We pulled up and parked next to a row of Harleys. "Bike Week is coming up," Velma said.

Velma and I got out of the car and made sure we lowered the windows a crack for Izzy who was snoring in the back. We made our way into the bar.

Like many other bars in Key West, Buried Money was an open-air bar. It was right near one of the major tourist attractions in Key West, a buoy, which claims to be the southernmost point in the contiguous United States. It is labeled as such and is one of the most photographed sites in Key West.

As we walked into the bar, I saw a large mahogany bar that encompassed most of the square footage of the room. The top of the bar was glass, and as I walked up to the bar, I could see it had gold doubloons, paper money, and other artifacts of pirate treasure on display. The bar was a history lesson in itself. I looked around for Charlie, and he was nowhere to be seen, so we sat and ordered a beer. Then Velma got busy talking to the bartender, I got up and walked around the bar.

As I walked around, I could see each part of the bar displayed a history of buried and sunken treasure, some still waiting to be found in the state of Florida. Apparently, there are two types of treasure, one requires a boat and extensive (expensive) diving gear and a lot of money. But the other, buried money, requires only a shovel, a metal detector, and lots of time and patience.

I read one display that caught my immediate attention.

"Another of Gasparilla's undiscovered treasures amounting to several million dollars was buried on an inlet somewhere south of St. Augustine. It has been stated that he never returned for the treasure."

Somewhere south of St. Augustine could be in the vicinity of Fish Camp, the former home of Pirate Pete where the convent now stands. This is no coincidence, I thought. I was learning more about my psychic ability.

It was relatively quiet, and Velma was still socializing with the bartender. Sister Matilda would love this bar, I thought, as I continued to walk around the large bar.

I saw a name that caught my eye, Blackbeard. Pirate Pete, according to Sister Matilda, was a descendant of the famous pirate.

"The pirate Blackbeard ruled the east coast of Florida and also buried a lot of his loot there."

It wasn't like they could set up bank accounts for their loot. I continued to read.

"A vast armada from Spain was struck by a catastrophic hurricane off Cape Canaveral in 1815. It is estimated that over $30,000,000 went down with 20 vessels. Some of the treasure still lies off the waters near the rocket pads of Cape Canaveral."

Fish Camp is not too far from Cape Canaveral, hmmm...$30,000,000...I thought and then almost jumped when Charlie came up to me and said, "A penny for your thoughts?"

"Geez, don't do that," I said as Charlie laughed and gave me one of his smiles that seemed like his eyes looked deep into my soul.

The next thing he did was a romantic kiss that ended with Velma and the bartender letting out some hooting and hollering.

As I recovered from his passionate greeting, Velma winked discreetly and said, "I am going out to check on Izzy. Be right back."

Charlie pointed to a table in a corner, "Let's sit back there, I like that spot because you can see everything coming and going. It's my favorite spot in the bar." Just as he was helping me into my seat, Velma returned, and he helped her as well.

"Thank you, Charlie, you are a true southern gentleman," Velma said.

"Let me go up to the bar and get refills for you two and a drink for me as well. I'll be right back," Charlie said as we both watched him make his way to the bar.

"My, oh my, he is still smitten with you, MC," Velma said. "All we need now is for Theo to walk in."

"Please Velma, let's not go there. Remember what we are here for. Let's just do that and go home," I said not believing a word.

Velma just gave me the "Yeah, sure look" as we watched Charlie make his way back with a round of drinks. We spent the next fifteen minutes or so catching up on the state of affairs with Charlie's boat, and he had the good sense not to bring up Theo. After a minute of silence, it was time to talk about Jennifer and her envelope.

I reached down and retrieved the envelope from my purse and handed it to Charlie who took out the paper and looked it over for a long while.

"I do remember when Harry told me about this," he said as he looked up at both of us and took a sip of his rum and coke.

"It was during tax season some years ago, and he and Jennifer were in the office to sign their joint return. He told both Jennifer and me that if anything ever happened to him, he would leave instructions for Jennifer in an envelope, and that envelope was to be delivered to me. Although it sounded kind of ominous at the time, I forgot about it until I heard he was killed," Charlie said looking straight at me and then back down at the paper.

He studied it for a few minutes and then said,

"This makes no sense. I was expecting something more financial in nature. What the hell is this? It looks like a crossword puzzle with maybe the Mona Lisa wearing a nun's habit?"

Good grief. He could see the nun, also.

"Look a little closer," I said, "at the puzzle."

With that, I watched as Charlie's eyes focused on the block of letters, and I saw the realization in his eyes when his brain connected the numbers as the coordinates for Key West.

"Damn, these numbers are the latitude and longitude for Key West," he said looking at me and then at Velma. I sat there quietly while Velma and Charlie both looked at the paper a little longer.

"Okay, so why would he leave the coordinates for Key West?" Charlie said to himself.

"As far as I can remember, he spent most of his time in Miami after he and Jennifer divorced. He loved to party in Fort Lauderdale and Key West."

"Yeah, and what's up with the nun who looks like Mona Lisa," Velma said.

Interesting, I thought, that both he and Velma could see the nun in the Mona Lisa, and I didn't see it until Sister Hildegard and Sister Matilda pointed it out to me. Charlie just stared at the paper and shrugged his shoulders.

"You don't see it?" I asked both Charlie and Velma.

"See what?" Charlie said and then paused while he looked back down at the puzzle paper.

"MC, do you see something no one else can see?"

Charlie was familiar with my DNA, and it spooked him a little, so I didn't bring it up much in conversation.

"I can see two words in the picture of the Mona Lisa," I said.

"Okay sweetheart, and what are those two words?" Charlie asked.

"Buried Money," I said, but while he and Velma took a minute to put two and two together, we all three looked up just in time to see my ex-husband, Theo, walk into the bar.

14

I hadn't seen Theo since my mother's funeral. During that difficult time, even though we were divorced he was there for my aunts and me, like a brilliant beacon in a darkening storm.

Theo spotted us and walked straight back to our table, straight over to me, and took my hands in his. I could see Charlie out of my peripheral vision watching me intently. He picked up his glass and downed his drink while Theo stood there for a minute and stared deep into my soul. He eventually let me go, but not before he kissed my hands.

"Hello, Mary Catherine," he said to me. He never called me by my nickname, always my full name. I watched as he walked over and gave Velma a big hug; they exchanged warm greetings. I looked over at Charlie who was looking at me. Theo walked over to Charlie, and like proper gentlemen, they shook hands.

Truce, their eyes said, at least for the moment.

"What are you drinking," Charlie said to Theo. "I'll order another round for the table."

"Let me get the next round," Theo said while I watched the two of them walk up to the bar together. They stood there chatting even after their drinks arrived.

As I watched them, I could see the bond that had existed between these two men who both periodically came into and out of my life, reappear. I knew I was part of the glue in that bond.

By the time they returned to our table, the renewed bond and alcohol had reduced the tension palpably. They laughed, joked, recalled memories, and good, old times. While I watched them, I got the feeling that they were very much like the pirates of old with gypsy souls. They were wanderers called to the sea by mermaids of the deep only they could hear.

The four of us drank and recalled old times, careful to keep the conversation and the elephants in the room at bay. Charlie had stuck the puzzle back in its envelope when Theo entered the bar. I only realized it was still sitting on the table like a bar fly listening in on our conversation when Theo looked down at the envelope and said, "What's that?"

"That, my old friend, is a mystery," Charlie said as he took the paper out of the envelope and showed it to him without saying anything more.

"Well, I see the coordinates for Key West and something that looks like the Mona Lisa," Theo said with a shrug of his shoulders as he stared at the paper a little longer. He handed the paper back to Charlie who laid it back down in the middle of the table.

"What's with all the pirate lore in this bar?" Velma asked.

"One of the original owners claimed to be a descendant of Blackbeard," Theo said. When I heard that I knew he was speaking of Pirate Pete.

"MC can actually see something in the Mona Lisa," Velma said pointing toward the paper in the middle of the table, and all eyes looked at me.

"Really," Theo said looking at me.

"You know your mother and your aunts are psychic. Don't tell me you have finally opened up to that, Mary Catherine."

"Well, what if I have?" I said to Theo, who had always encouraged me to keep an open mind and let it take me outside of the structured world where I felt most comfortable.

Theo was staring at me with the look that had always given me the feeling that he was the one who was psychic and could easily read my mind.

"Okay, yes, I have allowed my mind to explore my family DNA. I'm letting my guard down a little more these days," I said and watched a familiar smile appear on his face.

"So, you finally accept that you are psychic," Theo said while I took another drink of my beer.

"Yes, Theo," I said as I looked upward to the sky and my mother, "I accept it."

"Well, your mother must be happy," Theo said as he also looked upward and lifted his glass in a toast to her.

"Oh, I am sure she is," I said feeling her presence at the table, "as well as my two aunts. Now, if I would agree to join them on their public access TV show they would be ecstatic."

I looked down at the paper and picked it up.

"I can see the words Buried Money in the middle of the Mona Lisa," I said as I continued to stare at the paper and then placed it back on the table.

"Really," Theo said now also staring at the piece of paper.

"Yes, really," I said.

"Buried Money, as in the name of this bar?" Theo asked.

I nodded.

Theo picked up his drink and finished it and then leaned over the table, which seemed to direct the three of us to do the same.

"There has long been a rumor that this bar sits on buried money, a treasure buried long ago by pirates," Theo said.

"In fact, that owner I mentioned walked in here one day and said he was retiring. His ship had come in," Theo said.

"Then he walked out again, sold the bar, and was never heard from again. The subsequent owners of this bar kept the name Buried Money, kept alive the pirate feel, and spread the rumor that an owner had found some buried treasure," Theo said looking directly at me as a shiver shook its way up and down my spine.

"Are you okay?" he asked.

"Yes, fine," I said, thinking he was talking about Pirate Pete.

"I just felt a shiver run up and down my spine," I said as I felt the presence of the bar's history surrounding me.

"You know, my boat is strictly a research vessel, but I've been approached more than a few times by individuals who wanted to use the Mary Catherine to look for treasure off the coast of Florida. She has the capability to search for and locate items at depths much deeper than most treasure hunting vessels are capable of," Theo said.

"Were you ever approached by a man by the name of Harry Stone?" I asked out of the blue.

Theo just looked at me and then said, "You are psychic."

"Why do you say that?" Charlie now asked. "Did you ever meet him?"

"Yes, I have met him. Harry Stone was one that was very persistent. In fact, he called me again a few weeks ago offering me more money up front than I have ever been offered before to use the Mary Catherine on a treasure hunt. During that last call he even agreed that, in addition to the money, I could keep any artifacts. He assured me there would be artifacts. He sounded very urgent that last time he called."

"Just how much did he offer you?" Velma just had to ask while Charlie sat there looking at me and then at Velma.

"Enough," Theo said with a wink and a smile.

"And you turned him down?" Velma now said.

"No, this time I did not. The offer was too good to refuse since it could go a long way in funding my research. And then, when he added that I could keep the artifacts, I said yes and agreed to meet him here in Key West. He actually wanted to meet here, in this bar. But, I haven't heard from him since that last call."

"That's because he's dead," Charlie said and then revealed the nature of the piece of paper that was the center of our conversation.

Theo took it all in.

"I am sorry to hear that," Theo finally said, and then he looked at all three of us.

"What happened to him?" Theo asked.

"He was shot and killed in Miami," Charlie said.

Theo looked at him, quietly reflecting on what Charlie had just told him and then said, "The last time we talked, he told me he wouldn't need the use of the Mary Catherine very long because he knew exactly where to look. Like I said, he sounded very urgent. He told me that time was running out for him, and he needed to get this done."

"What did he mean? Time was running out, and he needed to get this done?" I asked.

"He didn't say, but in light of what you just told me, I'm wondering what he meant, also," Theo said.

"Did he tell you *how* he knew where to look?" I asked Theo.

"Yes, he said he had a map, which had been given to him by his grandfather who had first shown it to him when he was a kid. His grandfather told him pirate stories and also that they were descendants of a famous pirate, and that the map led to a treasure."

"Did he show you the map?"

"No, but he said he had it in a safe place. He said he would have it the next time we met."

"Really," I said thinking about Jennifer and Harry's locked storage room.

"He told me that we would not be using the Mary Catherine to search for the treasure. She was to serve as a decoy."

"Buried Money," I said looking at the puzzle paper sitting on the table, and as I did so, it moved ever so slightly.

15

We said our goodbyes and agreed to meet in the morning. Charlie went up to the bar and asked the bartender to call us a cab and paid him a few extra dollars so we could leave Velma's car parked at the bar. We walked outside to wait. Theo said he was walking back to the Galleon. But before he left, Theo pulled me aside and drew me very close to him. "I will always love you, Mary Catherine, and I am waiting for you, but we are not getting any younger. Time is no longer on our side. Let's not drag this into our next lifetime—again." I closed my eyes and breathed deeply as he kissed me. Then I watched as he walked down the street and into the dark.

"You are going to have to make up your mind," Velma said as she handed me Izzy in his crate while we stood waiting for the cab with our luggage. I looked down at Izzy, and

I swore he looked like he was nodding his head in agreement with Velma.

"Hush," I whispered to Izzy.

"If you don't decide between those two, you will be stuck right where you are, and time will pass you by. One day you will be an old lady sitting on your front porch looking back on an appointment you continued to cancel."

"An appointment?"

"Yeah, something my grandmother used to tell me growing up. Life is like a series of appointments, but the ones you put off making will haunt you at the end," Velma said.

The cab arrived and took us to Charlie's boat. I brought the luggage on board while Velma took Izzy and his crate and set him up a comfortable perch on the back of the boat. Velma and I sat down and admired a full moon shining over the water.

"What are you thinking?" Velma asked.

"About Harry and the treasure map?" I said, and Velma nodded.

"I think there is a treasure somewhere on land and not at sea, and that somehow the Sisters of Saint Anthony are part of this. The Mona Lisa is dressed in a habit, and the words I can see spelled out are 'Buried Money.' The coordinates for Key West are engraved on Pirate Pete's gravestone in the convent cemetery."

Velma looked at me and then said,

"MC, do you think Harry's death is also somehow tied into this Buried Money?"

"I don't know, but I do think something is going on, and we need to watch our backs," I said as Charlie began making his way onto the boat.

Velma and I both said our good-nights to Charlie, and he said he was staying up a little longer. We left him sitting next to Izzy. I heard him make his way down a little bit later, and then I dozed off into a deep sleep.

The next morning, Charlie, Velma and I met Theo for breakfast and the conversation remained light until we were getting ready to head out. I said one final good-bye to Theo. And then I watched him intently as he walked back to his boat.

Velma went for her car which Charlie had already loaded with our luggage and Izzy. During her absence, Charlie gave me a long kiss good-bye.

"I'm also waiting for you, Mary Catherine. At some point, you will have to make up your mind."

I looked at him, and then to avoid any further conversation in that direction, I reached down and pulled out the envelope with the intention of handing it over to him. He refused to take it saying, "No, I want you to keep it, and I want you to pay a visit to our dear friend, Jennifer, and find out what she's not telling us. Ask her about the treasure map. There's more to this story, and you need to get it out of her. Use your *genes*," Charlie said. "See you in a couple of days. I'll be waiting for that margarita." Then he turned away, and I watched as he walked off.

Velma and I retraced our drive north and stopped again for lunch at the bar in Marathon. We caught a break on the traffic through Dade County and made it home by midafternoon. I didn't say much on the trip home. Velma held up both ends of the conversation telling stories about her girls.

She dropped me off at the office. I drove my car home, had a light dinner and went to bed early. I knew I hadn't slept soundly because the next morning I was restless. I knew I had spent the night dreaming, but I couldn't for the life of me remember my dreams other than I was walking a long distance; I had the feeling I was trying to find my way home, but it was getting dark, very dark.

16

The next morning, I entered my office to find Velma at her desk and on the phone. I waved hello and walked back to my own space soaking in that comfortable feeling of safe and familiar surroundings. Soon the trip to Key West was out of sight and out of mind. I buried myself in my work, there was a lot of it to do, and it paid the bills.

After lunch, my mind did wander to Charlie, and I decided to text Jennifer and set up a time to meet her that evening after work. She texted back immediately and said to come over. She was at the house and was anxious to talk to me. I finished up the tax returns that were on my schedule for the day, and Velma took off to pick up the girls and take her mother to a doctor's appointment. I locked up the office and headed over to Jennifer's. I peeked into my purse, took another look at the envelope to make sure it was still there and headed out.

I arrived at Jennifer's to find full-scale pandemonium with Jennifer and Bruce front and center. Jennifer was dressed in her best Marilyn Monroe throwback outfit. She looked like a cross between a movie goddess and a hoochie mama for today's best gold digger look. "MC!" Jennifer said as she saw me. I walked over into the eye of the storm, and Bruce gave me a peck on each cheek. He looked me over, twirled me around, and said, "You might try Jennifer's new line of clothes, girlfriend." Then he turned and sashayed away.

"I'm going to have you try on my latest. It's more you, a mix between Lauren Bacall and the Audrey Hepburn look," Jennifer said.

"Really?" I said.

"How did you mix a line of clothing together with those two stars?" I said intrigued because I was a big fan of both.

"It's not clothing, it's wigs."

"Oh," I said as I followed Jennifer through the mansion out back to the deck with the magnificent view of the Atlantic Ocean. I decided to get right to the point, which wasn't hard since before we sat down I had a glass of wine and Jennifer got right to it.

"Well, what happened with Charlie? I heard Theo showed up in Key West." News travels fast in these circles.

"Yes, he did, and it was a little awkward with both Charlie and Theo together. But listen, right now I want to talk to you about the envelope and what Charlie had to say."

I took out the envelope and laid it on a nearby table. Jennifer picked it up, took out the piece of paper, looked at it, and put it back in the envelope.

"Okay," she said.

I could see in typical Jennifer fashion she wasn't going to volunteer any information, so I dove right into the deep end of the pool, which was dangerous since I wasn't a strong swimmer.

"Jennifer, did Harry ever talk to you about pirates and buried treasure?" I asked out of the blue not knowing what part of my brain that came from. It certainly wasn't how I had planned to start the conversation.

"Oh, Harry used to talk about it all the time," she said without the least hesitation.

"He was fascinated with the subject," she continued as she sipped her wine and looked out to sea.

"He used to sit right where you are and point out to sea and tell me that for all he knew, there was treasure buried right out there on our beach. He loved walking the beach with his metal detector, especially after a big storm."

"Did he ever mention a bar in Key West called Buried Money?" The question just popped out of the black hole located in my brain.

"Yes, his grandfather had owned that bar at one time and, when Harry was a kid, told him stories about being a descendant of the famous pirate, Blackbeard, and how he had buried treasure all over Florida. He even had a treasure map he used to show him as a kid."

"A treasure map, Jennifer? What was his grandfather's name?"

"Grover P. Stone, Harry used to call him Pirate Pete," she said.

I sat there mesmerized by what she had just said.

"Are you talking about the same person who left his estate to the Sisters of Saint Anthony?"

"Yes, Harry spent a lot of his youth there before his grandfather died. That's why he built this house. This part of Florida held happy memories for him. He used to say he had never been happier than in those days as a kid when he listened to his grandfather's stories about pirates."

"Why? Does that have something to do with this envelope? Is that what Charlie said? Is this a map to his grandfather's treasure?"

"I don't know. Did his grandfather tell Harry about a treasure?"

"Harry was just a kid when his grandfather died. But, Harry always believed his grandfather had found treasure."

I sat there for a minute, taking this all in, and as I did, I knew Jennifer still wasn't telling me everything. For some reason, the little girl from Kentucky was holding some cards back.

"Jennifer, what are you not telling me? Do you know where that treasure map is?"

She took a drink of wine, and a long sigh came from deep within her soul.

"I once saw something that looked like a treasure map. It was in Harry's storage unit. It was in a small wooden treasure chest. At the time, I didn't think anything of it. It just looked old."

She sat there for a few minutes sipping her wine. The IV dispensing information was slowly dripping.

"Harry locked the room with a combination lock and always used the same passwords, my dimensions, 38-24-36," she giggled. "Although I have to admit, the middle number might be a just little higher today. I checked the combination the other day when I found the empty envelope. Apparently, he changed it. It's sealed like a tomb."

"Jennifer, what do you remember about that map?"

"Just that it was old. I remember being very careful with it when I saw it and placed it back in the treasure chest."

I sat quietly for a moment. I could see she had something else to say but was choosing her words carefully.

"The map did have the words "Buried Money" written at the top. I remember that, and it definitely was a map of Florida."

"Buried Money," I said holding my breath. "Anything else?"

"Now that I am thinking about it, yeah, it had a big X on the map. Like marking where the treasure was buried."

"Do you remember where it was? You said it was a map of Florida."

"Wait here," she said.

Jennifer got up and came back with bar napkins and placed them on the table near us. I could see they were napkins from the bar Buried Money in Key West. It showed the state of Florida, and the location of the bar set out in the form of a treasure map.

"Harry loved that bar. He brought a stack of napkins and coasters back whenever he was in Key West."

Jennifer took a pen and drew an X on the napkin, and we both looked down at it. It was right below the bar, which would put it smack dab in the middle of the Navy installation in Key West.

"Wow," I said. "Your X is on government 'stay out of here, or we'll shoot you' property."

"So, what is going on? What did Charlie say?"

"He said he was in the dark as far as this puzzle Harry left. He asked me to talk to you, and see if you remember anything."

"That's about it," she said. "Well, at least I kept my promise. So, tell me about Theo."

"Well, Theo had been contacted by Harry to hunt down some treasure. He also told Theo he had a map."

"What? MC, maybe that was it, what Harry left behind in the envelope? Clues to the treasure and the map. I've really got to get into Harry's storage room now," Jennifer said. "If there is a treasure map, and it's still here, it's in that storage room."

I looked at the puzzle paper one more time while Jennifer watched.

"I just have a feeling that there is more to this. Maybe, if you can get in that room and find that treasure map, it will shed some more light."

***

Later, I woke up in the middle of the night after a bizarre dream that I could not remember, but I was sure it took place in Dreamland.

The investigative part of my brain started to lay out some facts. The contents of the envelope were missing, and Harry was dead. Was Harry murdered for the map or the location of the treasure? Or had Harry been in trouble and needed to find that treasure to get him out of a pickle? The psychic part of my brain said the latter.

I reached under my pillow, pulled out the paper, clicked on a light, and stared at the puzzle, and the Mona Lisa, who I now could see was dressed like a nun. Was that it? Was there treasure closer to home? Pirate Pete's home where the convent now sat? After all, Pirate Pete had left Key West and the bar, retired, bought a piece of property and built a mansion. If he had a treasure with him, it made sense that he would bury it on his own property or hide it in his mansion.

Did his grandfather's map show the location of treasure Pirate Pete had found? Was it in Key West and near where the naval air station now exists? Or did he bury the treasure on his property? The same piece of property he left to the Sisters of Saint Anthony? I sat there staring at the paper and fell sound asleep only to wake the next morning at dawn still holding the paper in my hand.

17

I got up, had some coffee, I went for my run and all the while my brain was thinking, ruminating, and attempting to process what I had learned. Afterward, I showered, dressed and drove to the office where I jumped into a busy day of meeting with clients, which I was thankful for because it gave my psychic brain cells a rest.

Later, in the afternoon, I pulled out my cell phone and found I had a text from Charlie saying he expected to be back early tomorrow. He wanted to get together the following night at Hotel Florida at the tiki bar where Ernie worked tending bar. I heard my cell buzz. I looked down, and it was Ernie, speak of the devil.

"MC, I heard from Charlie that you two would be stopping by the bar tomorrow," Ernie said.

"Yeah, he finally is getting back and texted me about meeting up."

"I also heard you and Velma had an interesting trip to Key West."

"Did we ever. I guess Charlie told you Theo also walked into Buried Money."

"Yeah, he told me a little bit about your run in. I hope you said hello to Theo from me."

Ernie knew Theo from the old days at the IRS, and like Charlie, they were guy pals.

"Have you been to Buried Money?"

"Oh yeah, lots of times, it's not too far from the Naval Air Station in Key West."

"I thought the Navy only had boats."

"Lots of people think that. Haven't you ever heard of the Blue Angels?"

"I have. Are they part of the Navy?"

"Yes, they are. The naval presence in the Keys was reduced in the 1970s. But, what wasn't overlooked was the fact that the location was superior for year-round flying weather and its strategic location since it was less than 100 miles from Cuba. The naval air station there is a state of the art training facility for air to air combat for military fighter aircraft. Theo has a number of Navy contracts."

"Theo runs a floating research facility. Not exactly fighter pilot training," I said.

"The air station is located near a national marine sanctuary. They work in partnership with the maritime community to protect Florida's eco-system."

"Oh, I see," I said. "A national marine sanctuary, I think I would enjoy visiting that."

"Oh, I am sure you would, and you would get the VIP treatment. Just ask Theo."

Theo again, was Ernie channeling my mother?

"Why the interest? Are you finally going to join Theo on that research ship and say good-bye to those financial statements?" Ernie asked. There it was again, Theo and me.

"Oh, nothing really, my interest was piqued while reading all that pirate history at Buried Money," I said.

"From what I've read, there could even be treasure right off of Key West, near the naval air station."

"Oh, I don't doubt there is treasure there and maybe even smack in the center of the naval air station. But no one will ever get onto government property to go treasure hunting. That area is well patrolled and heavily guarded, and besides even if you found anything, it would belong to the government."

"But they don't patrol the marine sanctuary?"

I could hear a moment of silence on Ernie's part.

"Got to go, see you tomorrow, MC."

Well, Ernie did have a point, I thought. Any treasure found in those parts would be difficult to locate, and then the government, state or federal, would lay claim. Unless you happened to have a research vessel named after you know who. Oh dear. No, I am not ready to go there, not just yet.

18

Just as I was settling in for another busy day, Velma popped into my office and said, "Sister Matilda called to say the bishop's office called and had asked Sister Hildegard and Sister Matilda to meet him and Sister Clarissa at the bishop's mansion."

"Did they say why they wanted the meeting?"

"To wrap up the audit," Velma responded.

"Wrap it up? They haven't even started," I said.

"Sister Matilda said Sister Hildegard wants to meet to go over some talking points, as she put it. She wants us at the meeting with Sister Clarissa."

We decided we could make it later that afternoon, and Velma called and set up a time with the sisters.

***

When we arrived, Sister Hildegard and Sister Matilda scooted us over to Pirate Pete's mansion, and as we entered, I assumed we were heading down to the bomb shelter. Instead, we followed the two nuns through the residence and out to a lanai. It reminded me a lot of Jennifer's lanai. In fact, as I walked through Pirate Pete's old home, I could see the similarity between this house and the house Harry Stone had built for Jennifer. Once settled down on some comfortable seating, Sister Matilda left us for a moment, and then returned with some wine and glasses.

"Nice," Velma said.

"Yes, church wine. It's holy," Sister Matilda responded with a slight wink.

The wine was poured, and once again Sister Matilda got up. She returned shortly with some snacks, which I recognized as Greek appetizers.

"Aunt Sophia and Aunt Anna were here the other day and left these snacks with us," Sister Matilda said.

No sooner had we taken a few sips of wine and a couple of appetizers when Sister Hildegard got down to business.

"We received a call from the bishop's office requesting our presence at a meeting with him and Sister Clarissa at his office. He wants to wrap up the audit."

"So, he's setting up this wrap-up meeting on his turf," Velma said.

"Yes," Sister Hildegard said.

"Have you been to his new *'Mansion by the Sea'*? I heard it was even bigger than the last one," I said.

"Only for the Christmas party he held last year. We made an appearance and then left. I was embarrassed to see the lavish house and food spread for the party. While our sisters were working to assist many who were down and out at Christmas, he wines and dines in extravagant luxury."

"You know, I think he actually lives a couple streets down from a wealthy client of mine," I said.

"Jennifer Stone?"

"Why yes, you've met her?"

"We have met her, she has been very kind, and a big supporter of women's issues," Sister Matilda said.

Interesting, I thought. Jennifer never mentioned that to me, but that little girl from Kentucky is very secretive.

"So here is what we need to go over before our meeting. We have it on good authority that Bishop Michael will be heading over to Rome to be part of the synod coming up next year," Sister Hildegard said.

Both Velma and I had a look of puzzlement on our faces at the mention of the word synod, which opened the door for Sister Matilda's history time. Sister Matilda had just drawn a large breath to begin speaking when Sister Hildegard cut her off at the pass.

"A synod is a gathering of the all, or I should say mostly all, male hierarchy of the Catholic Church. I say mostly male because they usually invite one or two token females."

"What do they do at the synod?" Velma asked.

"The leaders of the group, which would be Pope Benny and the Jets, will go over the latest hot button issues of the day and make sure all of them are on the same page."

"Like what?" Velma continued with a renewed interest in the Catholic Church.

"Well, one thing they won't be discussing is whether to offer communion to divorced and remarried Catholics or to craft more welcoming language for gays and lesbians," Sister Hildegard said.

"The only way such Catholics can remarry is if they receive an annulment, a ruling that says their first marriage never existed in the first place," Sister Matilda said with a big sigh.

"You're going to hell, MC," Velma said.

"What's the church's beef with gays and lesbians?" Velma asked.

"Well, let's see," Sister Hildegard said. "To put it bluntly, the traditionalist leaders of the church would tell you that homosexuality is 'intrinsically disordered,' and that same-sex unions could not 'remotely' be compared with "God's design for matrimony and family.""

"OMG," I said thinking about Bruce.

"Well, MC, it's not that different amongst right wing evangelists," Velma said.

"Getting back to our meeting with Bishop Michael and his auditor, Sister Clarissa," Sister Hildegard said. "You might hear these philosophical differences being discussed during our meeting. The Sisters of Saint Anthony falls on the progressive side of the church," Sister Hildegard said.

"Very progressive," Sister Matilda said.

"What exactly are you getting at?" I asked.

"MC, we are convinced that the purpose of this meeting is to let us know formally that the bishop, by orders of Cardinal Sole, intends to recommend disbanding our order because we are definitely not on the same page in the prayer book as these men, and we won't be anytime soon. I am not getting any younger, and I have come to the realization that I can no longer fly under the radar, nor do I intend to," Sister Hildegard said with a big nod from Sister Matilda.

"He can't do that, can he?" Velma asked.

"Technically, no. The bishop cannot, but if he has the backing of a powerful cardinal, it could be argued that he could. Plus, who could stop him? We are separate and independent. The truth of the matter is that we no longer have the funds to maintain the property the convent sits on and do the work of our calling. The parish churches in the diocese have been very kind and take up a collection each year for the order. We have used those funds to maintain the property. When the bishop's office called to set up the meeting, they also said the bishop regrets to tell us that there will be no such collection this year."

"Good grief," I said.

"What will happen? Where will you go?"

"We don't know, and for now have not spent a lot of energy on that thought. We may have to sell the convent property, but even with the proceeds, we might not be able to stay together as a group. We'll cross that bridge when we come to it, and hopefully, we won't have to."

"What a jerk," Velma saying out loud what we were all thinking.

"So, the Catholic Church does not take care of its nuns after everything the nuns have done for the church," I said.

"Yep," Sister Matilda said.

"We, unlike priests, have no retirement. We have just always pooled our money. We have no younger sisters coming along either. Because sisters are not ordained, they are considered part of the laity, not clergy, and therefore are not part of the hierarchical structure of the church. Religious orders, like ours, use the income from their ministries or rely on donations to financially support themselves. Most Catholics do not know that nuns are not financed by the Catholic Church."

Then as if I had a message from Saint Anthony it came to me.

"What if you found buried treasure?" I asked. "You could continue with your good works and not have to worry, even if they kick you out of the church. What if there is treasure buried right on the convent grounds? Left by Pirate Pete?"

Both Sister Hildegard and Sister Matilda were looking at me intently as if I had said something profound.

"Pirate Pete could have buried some treasure right here on the convent property. I'm sure you've thought as much yourself."

"We have but usually over a glass of church wine. Why child, you might have something there," Sister Hildegard said.

"That could explain why you were drawn into this puzzle. It seems to always circle back to Pirate Pete, our kind benefactor."

"Seems like it's time to get to work, Sister Matilda, time to go treasure hunting."

19

Sister Clarissa had just finished a meeting with the bishop. During the meeting, he made it abundantly clear that if the Sisters of Saint Anthony did not fall in line with time-honored church doctrine, the next step would be disbanding the order.

"We've already notified them that they are not getting a dime from any of the parishes in this diocese. That convent and the grounds require upkeep and maintenance, which doesn't come cheap," he said.

"Most of them are troublemaking old biddies. But don't worry, we will find nursing homes to take them in if it comes to that."

She was beside herself as he spoke to her in such a condescending manner. *Wait just a minute, aren't I a nun too. What will happen to me when I grow old? Thrown out like yesterday's leftovers?*

Sister Clarissa had no choice but to stuff her emotions, being as ambitious as the bishop. *I have been promised an invitation to the synod in Rome next year. That should put me on a level playing field with the bishop and many of the male religious leaders I deal with on a regular basis. After all, I am a Harvard lawyer too.*

He continued to drone on like she was his secretary.

When I think about things, I realize I actually agree with Sister Hildegard and her brood on many of their more liberal positions. But, there is no way I am going speak up and become the poster child for them. I am smarter than that. But...that doesn't mean that I can't help them from behind the scenes.

She was sure she could come up with a resolution that would work for all, and then she would present it to the bishop making him think it was his idea. That worked well with these narcissists that populate the hierarchy of the church. If not, she would pursue Plan B.

***

I decided to head over to Hotel Florida via Uber. Charlie had texted me that he was pulling into the marina and would meet me within the hour. When I got to the bar, I could see Ernie holding court with the usual group of regulars. He looked up and gave me a big smile, and as I sat down at the bar brought me a cold beer.

"Charlie is on his way," Ernie said. "And…so how is the Mary Catherine?"

"I assume she is holding up," I said. "I haven't been on board for a few years."

"What exactly does Theo do on that ship?" I asked Ernie.

"He's always told me that the Mary Catherine is an Environmental Research Vessel, whatever that means, but then he also works with the Navy in the Keys."

Ernie looked at me with his spook look.

"I remember that Theo bought the Mary Catherine from the Cayman Islands government just before they tried to sink it and use it for a scuba diving attraction. It had evidently been used for drug smuggling and before that, it was a US Navy light cargo ship that had been decommissioned."

"And what was a *light cargo ship* used for by the United States Navy?" My brain asked Ernie without any help from my thought process.

"During the 1960s, it was a technical research ship used by the Navy to gather intelligence by monitoring, recording and analyzing electronic communications from nations all over the world."

"Okay," I said.

"To put it simply, in another life, the Mary Catherine was a spy ship."

"Why am I not surprised by all this?" I asked.

"At the time these ships were active, the mission of the ships was covert observation. The public was told that the ship was conducting research into atmospheric and communications phenomena. The actual mission was secret. So, the ships were commonly referred to as spy ships."

"So, what is it now, a spy ship or a research vessel?"

"You might want to ask Theo that the next time you see him, and then let me know. I've been wondering about that very question myself," Ernie said as he went to take some orders at the bar for a group of bikers who had just arrived.

I sat on my stool drinking my beer and thinking about the Mary Catherine. "A spy ship," I said to no one in particular. Ernie came back and placed a cold beer next to me, and before I could turn around Charlie was sitting beside me.

"Hello, beautiful," he said.

I looked at him, and he leaned over and gave me a welcoming kiss.

"Ernie, my man, how are you?"

"No complaints, Charlie, and you?"

They spent a few minutes catching up, which gave me an opportunity to reflect on these two guys that had been part of my life for a long time.

Charlie was a good friend, and without a doubt, he would be happy to accelerate the friendship. But I knew in my heart that whenever I thought about a lasting relationship, my thoughts returned to Theo. The problem was Theo meant jumping on board, literally.

"So, MC, did you speak to Jennifer?" Charlie asked.

Before I could answer, I noticed that everyone at the bar, especially the bikers, was looking at something behind me. Ernie looked as if he were mesmerized, so Charlie and I turned around to see none other than Jennifer Stone arriving in style in a stretch limo with all the trimmings. She was dressed like her idols, Dolly and Marilyn. Every male eye at the bar was focused like radar on her boobs, which bounced in time to a tune only Jennifer could play on the guitar she was toting.

"Jennifer," I said. "What brings you here?"

I looked at Ernie who was frozen still like a statue. I had to take a closer look to make sure he had not stopped breathing or about to go into cardiac arrest. Here was a man who, at one point, had the president's private phone number, but around Jennifer, he was a school kid with a serious crush.

"Happen to be driving by and thought I'd drop in, and if the handsome bartender was in agreement, I'd sing a few tunes."

Ernie came to life but still could not articulate any words. He was only capable of smiling and nodding his head up and down, like a bobblehead.

"I think that's a yes," I said looking at Charlie who was giving me a knowing smile.

"Sweetheart, could you get me a Cosmo?"

"Y-y-y-yes ma'am, on the house," Ernie said and caught himself tripping over his feet to get the drink for Jennifer.

"Charlie, how are you?" Jennifer said as she sat on a bar stool diagonally from the two of us.

"Fine, and you Jennifer?"

I could see Charlie was also taken by Jennifer's beauty, but I could also see his brain working. I knew where the conversation would eventually go, so I decided to get to the bottom line.

"Charlie was just asking me if we had talked," I said looking at Charlie and then Jennifer, who was quiet for a moment, but I could tell she knew what I meant.

"To be honest, I had my driver stop hoping that you both would be here so we could talk," she said while flashing her movie star smile at Ernie who delivered the Cosmo and parked himself close by to be at her beck and call. He had now turned into a puppy, Jennifer's puppy.

The bikers across the bar were still watching her while they sipped their beers. She smiled their way, and I thought they were all going to fall off their bar stools. The leader of the pack started to get up and head over to our side of the bar, but stopped cold when Ernie gave him the *Dirty Harry* "are you feeling lucky?" look. His friends pulled him back and sat him down with his beer.

We all watched as Jennifer put down her Cosmo and reached for her guitar. Out of its belly, she pulled out an envelope. Great, I thought, another envelope.

"After we had talked, MC, I went back and rechecked that combination I spoke of," she said looking directly at me. "After many tries, I found the one that worked, and then I found this." She handed the envelope to Charlie.

"I'm sure Harry would want you to look at this," she said watching Charlie and taking a sip of her Cosmo.

"This is a copy. The original is very old, and I have it in a safe location."

I just stared at her and whispered, "You figured out the combination?" She nodded her head yes. I then watched as Charlie opened the envelope and took out a copy of what looked like a very old treasure map. As

I looked at it, I felt like I recognized it, and for a minute, I was taken back to another time. For a split second, the feeling came over me that we were all pirates looking at a treasure map. I could see the map was exactly as Jennifer had described it with the big fat X a little south of the bar, Buried Money.

Jennifer continued, "This map belonged to Harry's grandfather, whom everyone called Pirate Pete. He used to show Harry this map when he was a kid. He told him that this map had been passed down from Blackbeard and that Harry was a direct descendant of Blackbeard."

Charlie was studying the map and gestured for Ernie to take a look, which he did reluctantly since it would require him to take his eyes off of Jennifer. Ernie finally looked at the map, which Charlie had carefully placed on the bar so Ernie could see it. Spook Ernie came to life.

"The X is smack dab on the naval air station. If that's where Blackbeard buried his treasure, good luck because there is no way the Navy is going to allow anyone on their property to look for treasure. Unless, of course, you claim to be archeologists or own a research vessel," he said laughing. We all, of course, were seriously considering his words.

"That was a joke," he said looking at me. "Don't even go there."

We all continued to stare at the map. Charlie eventually turned to me and said, "MC, would you hold this map and see if you can call on your ability? Maybe it will tell you something. You seem to have seen something in the other puzzle piece Harry left for me."

I knew what Charlie was asking. I looked over at Jennifer, who was looking at me and nodding her head in agreement. I suspect she had also had this in mind when she had decided to drop by the bar.

"Okay," I said as I took the map from the bar and held it in my hands. I closed my eyes and didn't feel a thing.

Then, as I waited, my mind drifted back to a couple of days ago to the cemetery and to the spot where Pirate Pete was buried. This was the way my psychic ability worked. It was as if I was recalling a memory and sometimes when it happened, I needed to decipher the message. I opened my eyes.

"Anything?" Charlie said.

"Actually, all I could see was the cemetery at the convent and a gravestone. It's where Harry's grandfather is buried."

"You could see that?" Jennifer said.

"Well, it's not like it was a vision. I was there a few nights ago when I was meeting with the sisters. We were walking on the convent grounds, and we ended up in the cemetery. Sister Hildegard and Sister Matilda showed me where Harry's grandfather is buried. He left everything to them in return for a prime spot in the convent cemetery."

"Interesting," Ernie said.

"So, MC, maybe your psychic genes are telling us the treasure is on the property where the convent now sits," Jennifer said.

"Yeah, maybe, and that brings us to this," I said.

"You remember Bishop Michael?" I said to Charlie who rolled his eyes and looked over at Ernie who closed his eyes. All three of them had prior dealings with the bishop and his brother, Walther, thanks to Velma and me.

I continued, "Anyway, he has been chosen by the Vatican to reform the ways of the Sisters of Saint Anthony, who are a little too progressive for his strict interpretation of the church doctrine. The Sisters are calling it an audit and have asked for my help. They are not backing down, and he is threatening to disband their order, which would lead to the closing down of the convent. He has the backing of some high up cardinal in the Vatican, so it is serious."

"He can't do that," Jennifer interjected.

"They do fantastic work. I won't allow that to happen," Jennifer said.

"Getting back to the map," Ernie said trying to refocus the conversation.

"Is there anything else that psychic ability of yours is telling you?"

"I'm not so sure it's my psychic ability or just putting all the pieces of the puzzle together. But, I do feel like there is treasure out there, somewhere. Could be in the Keys, or maybe closer."

I gave the map back to Charlie. What I didn't tell them was that Sister Hildegard and Sister Matilda were already out there with their shovels and metal detectors.

Charlie was holding the map now and said,

"Theo told us that Harry had contacted him to ask for the Mary Catherine to look for treasure, and he had told Theo he knew exactly where to look. He had a map. This must be the map, passed down from the pirate, Blackbeard, to his descendants."

"Harry was after this treasure, but why now? He's had that map for a long time," I said.

"Maybe he needed the money to pay somebody off," Jennifer said.

We all turned to look at Jennifer, "Is there something else you haven't told us?" I asked. When she looked at me, I knew she was now going to tell us something she had not told anyone else. When she started talking she looked directly at Ernie.

"I think I know why he was killed. He was involved in a lot of deals and had always told me to be safe it was better I didn't know any of the details. He came by the house a few weeks before he…was killed. He was very solemn and spent some time in that room he still used for personal storage," she said looking at me.

"Before he left, he said good-bye and told me he might not see me again. That he had gotten in too deep this time with some very dangerous men, who had lost a lot of money as a result of an investment he had placed them in. The detective who called me to tell me that Harry had been killed later called me again and told me they suspected Harry was killed because he somehow had gotten involved with money laundering. I think he was going to look for his grandfather's treasure to pay off whoever killed him."

"Let me do a little investigating on my own," Ernie said, as I looked over at Jennifer who was looking at Ernie with her beautiful eyes. She smiled at him.

"Thank you, Ernie, it would bring me some peace," was all she had to say to have Ernie and his many covert contacts at her disposal. Like I said, the little girl from Kentucky was no dummy.

20

We adjourned to Charlie's boat. Ernie joined us after he finished up at Hotel Florida. After a few drinks, we called it a night. We didn't talk much more about the treasure map. Jennifer, her job done, left it with Charlie, who handed it to me.

"Sleep on this," he said as he gave me a kiss good-bye.

Jennifer offered me a ride home in the limo, which I accepted.

"So, you were able to open Harry's storage room?" I had to ask.

"I had to. I kept trying various combinations and finally hit on one that worked," Jennifer said.

"Was the map where you remembered?"

"Yes. It was in the treasure chest just like the last time I saw it."

I waited to see if Jennifer was going to reveal any new information. It was killing me to do so, but I kept quiet.

"That's all that was in the room," she said. "The room was empty. The treasure chest and map were the only items in there. I think he removed whatever else he kept there a long time ago and just kept that room to keep the map," she said.

"I wonder why he didn't take the map with him the last time he came for a visit."

"Oh, I think he did. I now remember that he used the copy machine in my office while he was there. He probably made a copy and placed the original back in his safe room. My guess is that is why his apartment was ransacked when he was killed. Whoever killed him was probably looking for the original map."

Right before she dropped me off, she said, "If any treasure is found on convent property it will belong to the sisters. Correct?"

"Well, I suppose it would belong to the sisters if it is found on convent property," I said. "I would say they should keep it quiet, though."

"I agree," Jennifer said.

"I am sure it would be what his grandfather would want. If he buried the treasure on the property and left it to the sisters, then I would say that would have been his wish. He was Catholic, you know, and in the end wanted to be buried in a Catholic cemetery."

"Yes, I had heard that he bribed Saint Anthony," I said.

Jennifer looked at me puzzled.

"I'll explain it to you the next time we meet for wine. It's a long story."

"So, what do your psychic genes tell you?"

I looked at Jennifer. It was as if the memory was clearing when she asked that question.

"Jennifer, I think, for whatever reason, Harry was after treasure left behind by his famous ancestor. The treasure map shows a big X on Navy property. He contacted Theo who also works with the Navy, so maybe the treasure is in the Keys. Theo would never agree to trespass on Navy property, but it could be the treasure was nearby in water located in and around the Florida Keys National Marine Sanctuary."

Jennifer looked at me and then started to say something. But then I could see she changed her mind and instead said,

"By the way, my security team found another bug in my house."

"They did?" I said after a moment of silence and a hard stare, just to make my point that her way of dispensing information was becoming a bit annoying.

"Yes, they said it was different from the other bug. It looked to them like something the government currently uses."

"Government?"

"My security team has a broad background," Jennifer said as she reached into her guitar case, pulled out the bug, and handed it over to me. Maybe you could show it to Ernie."

"Why didn't you show it to him tonight?" I asked.

"Didn't want to overload him," she said. "You need to learn that about men, MC. You've got to be patient." She looked at me as we pulled up to my condo and said, "Have a good night's sleep. We'll talk in the morning."

I literally did have a good night's sleep. I stuck the bug and the treasure map in my pillowcase along with all the other stash and fell soundly asleep. Luckily the next day was a Saturday, and I had the luxury of sleeping a little later.

21

While drinking my coffee the next morning and thinking about dropping in to see my aunts, my cell rang and without thinking to see who was calling, I answered it.

"Good morning, Mary Catherine. This is Sister Clarissa. I was wondering if you could meet me for lunch. I'd like to talk to you in the spirit of finding a resolution to this audit, as the sisters are calling it. You and I are trained to find compromises that lead to fair settlements for all parties," she said. Will one o'clock work for you?"

Something told me to say yes, so in my half-awake state I agreed, and we settled on a spot to meet.

I finished my coffee, showered, dressed, hopped into my car, and drove to where we had agreed to meet. Neutral territory, I thought, a favorite spot on the water in Boca

Vista. I entered the restaurant, looked around and then spotted Sister Clarissa. I made my way over to her booth which had a delightful view of the Intracoastal and boat traffic.

"Thank you, Mary Catherine, for agreeing to meet with me today. I do appreciate your willingness to do so," she said as she reached out to shake my hand. She looked more like one of the wealthy socialites that populate the town of Boca Vista than a nun.

"Of course," I said. "Please call me MC."

"Mary Catherine is such a beautiful name," she said with an uncharacteristically perky smile.

We spent the next ten minutes chatting and deciding what we were going to order for lunch. I noticed that Sister Clarissa ordered a salad with the dressing on the side. Figured that's probably all she ate to keep that trim.

Before long, though, we started talking fitness, and the time flew while she told me about her efforts to stay fit and how she worked at it religiously, her words not mine. I had actually begun to enjoy the lunch, but when it was time to get down to business, I could see her demeanor change.

"Mary Catherine, I have given it some prayer and additional thought, and I am now willing to concede that you probably are the one that may be able to intercede on behalf of the good sisters and the bishop to resolve this matter. Not unlike your role with the IRS," she said with a million-dollar smile or one that certainly cost a few dollars.

As I sat there listening, I could tell once again she had carefully crafted the words she used as if she was speaking to a jury. I recalled Sister Hildegard warning me that Sister Clarissa was suspected of having powers of her own in addition to being a skilled and highly trained lawyer.

"She was used to swimming with sharks and waiting for the right moment to strike," Sister Hildegard had said.

"I think we all know that you and the good sisters have some unique abilities," she said looking directly at me and then out at the water. There it was, out of the closet. I sat there quietly and waited for her to continue.

"We also know that the sisters march to a different drummer than that of the bishop. It's all good. Just between the two of us, I admire the sisters for their good works," she said and then another pause, while she looked again out at the water where we could see a large boat motor by the restaurant.

"With that said, I implore you to speak to them and see if they would agree to, let's say, modify their work so that it falls in line with the bishop's more conservative interpretation of church doctrine. I'm sure they can find many beneficial projects. Talk to them about dropping these other controversial projects they have championed, at least for a while, until this audit business blows over. If they would agree, I am sure, when I speak to the bishop, I can convince him to end this audit on terms that are satisfactory to the sisters. They can go about their business, and the bishop would leave them be. Later they can slowly return to their more liberal ways," she said. "Not to the same extent, of course, but you know what I mean. Will you speak to them?"

"Just so I am clear, Sister Clarissa. You are asking me to speak to them and get them to agree to drop all their current work that doesn't line up with the strict teachings of the church?"

"Yes," she said, "precisely. This would allow the bishop to shine in front of his newfound friend, Cardinal Sole, and Cardinal Sole would look good back at the Vatican. For now, ask them to move these projects to an inactive status," she said now looking back out on the water and then straight back at me.

"One more thing they would have to agree to. The bishop is planning a press conference for the media with the announcement of a list of his traditional projects he has lined up this year for the diocese. I would like to tell the bishop that Sister Hildegard will be there with him when he makes that announcement. Just for the press," she said.

"A press conference?"

"Yes, like I said. It would allow the bishop to publicly announce the favorable conclusion of the audit. It is starting to make some unpleasant waves in the community. He wants to get it done soon."

We both took a minute to replay what we had just talked about in our heads, making sure we heard the same thing and understood the fine print. The press conference for the media would certainly put the nix on the interview Aunt Sophia did with Sister Hildegard.

"Sister Clarissa, I will speak to Sister Hildegard in the spirit of negotiating a resolution to this audit. However, between the two of us, I can tell you they will not agree to this proposition. To do so, they would be turning their back on far too many people that have come to rely on their help. This does not sound like a settlement. It sounds more like a concession on the part of the sisters." I watched as Sister Clarissa once again was staring out at the water and the boat traffic.

"All right, Mary Catherine, have it your way. I tried." The Sister Clarissa I had come to know had returned.

"A concession, yes maybe so, Mary Catherine. The bishop is a very powerful and ambitious man," she said now, very seriously. "Please also know this," she said. "The sisters are a roadblock standing squarely in the road that leads to the bishop's ultimate goal."

She leaned forward a bit and lowered her voice to an almost ominous tone, "In words you can understand, let's just say they have no choice but to concede. He is holding all the cards."

My backbone rose it its full height, and I responded, "Excuse me, Sister Clarissa, I would counter that it depends on who is reading those cards." I might have been born at night, but it wasn't last night.

"Those cards spell disaster for those nuns, Mary Catherine," she said now in a softer tone.

"Are you implying that he will go through with his threats to close down the order and force them to sell the convent property?"

"He has the power to do so. He has the backing of Cardinal Sole. However, he won't have to go that far. He already has what he needs to force them to sell that property."

"What are you talking about? Then without waiting for her to respond, I asked her, "Sister Clarissa, is there something on that convent property that the bishop wants?" My psychic genes were ablaze. Locking horns with Sister Clarissa had certainly struck the match.

She stopped and looked at me or at my mind and then closed her eyes.

"Look, I don't know what might or might not be on that property, but I do feel the cardinal is after the convent property for reasons other than the audit. I don't know why. Since I'm just a woman, the bishop and the cardinal don't share their secrets with me. I am only telling you this because I share common bonds with the sisters. I am imploring you to listen to me and trust me when I say they need to fall in line with the bishop—for now. This will all blow over, at some point. Trust me on this. If they don't the bishop has authorized me to start foreclosure proceedings on the convent property. In six months, they will be disbanded and put out to pasture in who knows what nursing homes."

"Foreclosure? What are you talking about, Sister Clarissa? What does he have on the sisters?" I asked.

Despite her passionate plea, I kept hearing Sister Hildegard's voice. "Watch her. She will try to play with your mind."

Sister Clarissa reached into her expensive purse, which was worth more than my car and pulled out a document and handed it to me.

"This copy is for Sister Hildegard as Mother Superior. I also made a copy for you," she said like she had done me a big favor.

I took a look at the document she handed me.

"What is this, Sister Clarissa?"

"The bishop was going to explain this when we met with Sister Hildegard about concluding the audit, but in light of our meeting today, I have decided to give you and Sister Hildegard a heads up," she said smugly.

"According to the bishop, this document represents a loan the diocese made to the order many years ago. A few years before Sister Hildegard became Mother Superior, and a little before he arrived as a new bishop, the convent was in need of a loan. The mother superior of the order at the time approached the diocese," Sister Clarissa said.

"When the Bishop arrived, he was told about the loan, and that the diocese holds a lien on the property. As you know, this gives the bishop, or I should say the diocese, the right to foreclose on the property in the event the order defaults on the loan."

I quickly looked at the paper Sister Clarissa handed me. It appeared to be a loan between the Order of the Sisters of Saint Anthony and the diocese.

"Was a lien recorded?" I asked.

"I'm sure it was," Sister Clarissa replied. Typical lawyer talk for maybe it was, or maybe it wasn't, I thought.

"As a lawyer, what I can tell you is that the document gives the diocese the footing to start foreclosure proceedings on the convent property on the basis that the loan has defaulted," Sister Clarissa said.

"Has he discussed this loan and the fact that you say it's in default with Sister Hildegard?"

"It's my understanding he has not. He has been aware of this for a long time, but has left it alone figuring that the diocese would eventually be repaid," Sister Clarissa said.

"As a CPA and someone who used to work for the IRS, I can tell you that I'm a little suspicious about the timing of this document *and* whether or not this is, in fact, a valid document."

"Are you saying the bishop fabricated this document?" Sister Clarissa said with a good show of real disbelief in her voice.

"Sister Clarissa, you said so this very afternoon that the bishop is a blindly ambitious man and now with the cardinal behind him, he will do whatever is necessary to further his goals. You have to agree that the timing of this document is suspect."

I could see Sister Clarissa was mulling over my words. She may have thought the same thing herself, but in true lawyerly fashion, she was not about to admit it.

I continued, "With that said, I would be inclined to agree with you *if* a lien was recorded by the diocese at the time of the loan. Don't you think it's odd that the bishop did not have a copy of that lien in his files along with this loan document?"

Sister Clarissa did not flinch. She just shrugged her shoulders.

"So, you are telling me the bishop, on behalf of the diocese, intends to foreclose on the convent property unless he gets his way?"

"What I am telling you is that the bishop has instructed me to start the proceedings if the audit is not resolved in such a manner that he is confident that the good sisters will follow church doctrine on a more conservative basis," she said.

"He has the full backing of the cardinal if it comes to that. I have talked to the bishop, and I do believe he would agree to the settlement I laid out today. It would give the sisters a little more time, especially if the bishop continues to rise in the ranks of the church hierarchy," she said.

She looked placidly at me, took a quick breath, leaned forward a bit, and then continued in a quieter tone, "Frankly, if they bide their time, he probably will be gone within a year, off to Rome with the rest of the good old boys."

I had to admit she was good, and I felt her pulling me into her way of thinking. I had to get out of here before she managed to talk me into something I would later regret. Sister Hildegard was right; she had strong powers of her own.

"Sister Clarissa, I appreciate you bringing this matter to my attention. I will speak to the sisters and get back to you. I will also let you know the outcome of my courthouse search, which I plan to do first thing Monday morning."

I could see the lunch was coming to an end, and Sister Clarissa was getting ready to leave.

"So how much is this loan in arrears?"

"The loan itself was for $10,000, but over time and with the accumulation of interest on the unpaid amount, it's currently equal to about what the property is worth—according to the bishop. He plans to forgive the interest and declare the principal paid in return if Sister Hildegard agrees to buckle down and follow a more conservative approach to their work.

"No more counseling young women on birth control, passing out condoms, or using the convent as a women's shelter. No more advocating for liberal ideas and social changes, which have no foundation or basis in the traditional teachings of the Catholic Church. In short, no more feisty nuns," Sister Clarissa said as she got up to leave.

"He wants to show the Cardinal that they have turned over a new leaf."

My psychic genes were on fire, and I had to ask before she left,

"Tell me, Sister Clarissa, was this Cardinal Sole's idea? This mysterious loan that appears out of the blue? I can see that the bishop is caught between a rock and a hard place and is going along with this charade. I believe there is something on the convent property that the cardinal wants," I said. Without even thinking I grabbed her arm and immediately felt a shiver. I knew my words were true.

"Mary Catherine," she said as I released her arm. She leaned very close to me and with both hands grabbed my shoulders and whispered,

"You are new at this game. Be careful with your gift."

She now stood model straight and flashed that perfect smile.

"I appreciate your time, and I look forward to hearing from you."

With that, she walked out of the restaurant and stiffed me for the lunch.

22

I immediately called Sister Hildegard and told her I was heading over to the convent and needed to speak to her. When I got there, she ushered me right into her office. Sister Matilda was waiting there and pointed to the chair next to her. Sister Hildegard sat down behind her desk and gave me the nod to begin.

"Sister Clarissa called me today and invited me to lunch. I decided to meet her and see what was up her sleeve. She showed me this." I handed the copy of the loan document to Sister Hildegard.

"Are you familiar with this?"

Sister Hildegard looked at it and then handed it to Sister Matilda. After a few minutes of study on Sister Matilda's part, she shook her head no and handed the paperwork back to Sister Hildegard who then spoke.

"No, I've never seen this before. I do recall when I first arrived, the outgoing Mother Superior went over the books and records of the order, but there was no mention of a loan by the diocese. This is a fabrication the bishop is trying to scare us with," Sister Hildegard said tossing the loan document onto her desk.

"I think it's more likely the cardinal," I said and relayed the conversation with Sister Clarissa and the weird mind games Sister Clarissa played out during our luncheon.

"I see," Sister Hildegard said.

"I warned you she has a powerful mind and uses it to great advantage. You should be careful, Mary Catherine, when challenging someone like Sister Clarissa. From time immemorial, people like her have played with the minds of their adversaries and attempted to convince them that they are their friends," Sister Hildegard said with an ominous tone to her voice. "That is what she is trying to do to you."

"And she will stab you in the back," Sister Matilda added and then raised an invisible knife and took a couple of jabs at Sister Hildegard's desk. She made some noises that reminded me of the movie *Psycho* to make sure I got the point.

"Literally, not figuratively," Sister Matilda said and took a couple more jabs at the desk. Sister Hildegard closed her eyes and whispered, "Mother of God, help me."

I stifled a chuckle and closed my eyes for a moment and then took in a deep breath.

"I understand the bishop's motives, but why would the cardinal be after the convent property?"

"I don't know," Sister Hildegard said.

"But what I do know is that all these events are circulating around you like a water spout. You are the one that can search out the answers to that question and all the others."

"Why me?" I asked them.

"We don't know, dear. We've been asking ourselves that same question for some time now," Sister Hildegard said.

"You do seem to attract these events," Sister Matilda added, preaching to the choir.

I closed my eyes again and took another deep breath.

"Are you saying that Jennifer's puzzle, Pirate Pete's treasure, the bishop, and the cardinal are all tied together?"

"Yes, I would say so," Sister Hildegard said.

"It may all have something to do with the convent property. It could be treasure or something altogether different. Something has happened. A catalyst went off and sparked the hunt for whatever is buried on this land, and it is seeking you out."

"Okay, Okay," I said feeling a headache coming on from the glasses of wine shared with Sister Clarissa over lunch.

"Monday, I will go down to the courthouse and see if a lien for this loan was recorded.

According to Sister Clarissa, the loan is in default. Is there any way you can speak with the previous mother superior?"

"Only if we hold a séance," Sister Hildegard said. "She is buried in our cemetery."

"Let's hold off on that for now," I said seeing that Sister Hildegard was not joking.

"Did she say how much we owe?" Sister Matilda asked.

"She said that the full amount is equivalent to the current worth of the convent property and that most of that is interest. Sister Clarissa said that the bishop is willing to forgive the interest and call the loan paid in full if you would all agree to behave."

"Of course, he would. He is such a kind and benevolent soul; don't you agree Sister Matilda?"

"Oh yes, Mother Superior. Right up there with his new best bud, the cardinal."

"That's not all. Sister Clarissa said part of the deal is that he wants you to appear with him at a press conference. He intends to show your new and more compliant side."

"I see. The good bishop, with the backing of his new friend, is playing dirty," Sister Hildegard said while rising to her full six feet and starting to pace the room while fumbling with her basketball size rosary beads, which was wound around her waist like a belt.

"I sincerely doubt that this document would hold up in court, but I'm afraid it's enough to start the foreclosure proceedings," I said.

I watched Sister Hildegard as she turned to face me and heard a tiny sound from Sister Matilda who I could see out of the corner of my eye was holding her breath.

"I think you should supply him with his very own signed and autographed copy of the interview, which your Aunt Sophia can't wait to air on public access TV. Tell the good bishop that we will not be blackmailed," Sister Hildegard said as she walked over and sat at her desk. She pulled out a DVD, signed the case, and handed it to me. I looked down at the label, and it was titled "Feisty Nuns."

"Are you sure this is the road you want to take?" I asked holding up the DVD.

"Absolutely," Sister Hildegard answered without missing a beat.

"MC, we have been on that road for a long time, and there will be no turning back."

"In that case, I'll be happy to deliver this to the good bishop this afternoon."

"Did he give us a deadline?" Sister Matilda asked with a worried look on her face realizing the significance and consequences of Sister Hildegard's decision.

"Yeah, pretty much yesterday," I said.

"We really need to find Pirate Pete's treasure," Sister Matilda said to Sister Hildegard as she got up and rolled up her sleeves.

"Have you been looking?"

"Oh, yes. All over the place and we have dispatched all the sisters to look. We'll pick up our pace now."

"Look behind the large credenza in the bomb shelter," I said out of nowhere.

Sister Hildegard and Sister Matilda stared at me and then said in unison,

"We will. Your psychic abilities are getting stronger. For now, we will take any measures we can to continue to delay this new phase of the audit. I am hearing rumors that a new pope may be around the corner," Sister Hildegard said with a big smile.

"How are you hearing this?"

"We have friends in high places, too. Go, you need to deliver that DVD. Trust me, it will stall the bishop's plans, and in the meantime, we'll keep looking for the treasure."

"This is a charade," I said pointing to the loan document.

"No worries. This whole thing has been an eye opener. We have plans for some projects for any treasure we may find."

"And what might they be?" I said as they both got up and walked me to the door.

"For one, we are going to turn the convent into a residence for older nuns. We are getting older, and this whole thing with the bishop got me thinking. A lot of our older nuns have no place to go," Sister Hildegard said.

"Like an assisted living facility," Sister Matilda said.

"In fact, we plan to pair the young women who come through our doors with a mentor. Many of these older nuns have led extraordinary lives, can teach from the wisdom of experience, and still have a lot to give."

"That sounds fantastic," I said as I reached the front door.

"We also plan to have an even bigger herb garden," Sister Matilda said.

"Yes, we have plans to expand the garden of Saint Hildegard. It must be ready to start selling our medicinal herbs when the time comes," Sister Matilda said with a wink.

"That will go a long way toward bringing in needed revenue for the order in the event the bishop and cardinal do kick us out of the church," Sister Hildegard said.

"Oh my," I said.

"We'll need your help with the books," Sister Matilda said with a big smile as I waved good-bye and left the convent to make the drive to the bishop's mansion.

Wonderful, I thought, as I made the drive and thought about these nuns as my clients. I will blow that bridge up when I come to it.

The butler answered the front door along with Sister Clarissa.

"That was quick," she said.

"I have spoken to the sisters, and I have a message for the bishop," I said as Sister Clarissa stood in the doorway. I handed her the autographed copy of the DVD.

"Ask the bishop to watch this interview of Sister Hildegard. It will appear on public access TV and hit the newsstands if he proceeds with this foreclosure. He should find it very interesting."

Sister Clarissa took the DVD and then said, "I will." She moved closer to me and whispered in my ear, "Tell the sisters I'm rooting for them. Just doing my job, nothing personal, it's just business."

We shook hands, and I left with a smile on my face, got to love those nuns.

***

Cardinal Sole looked up from his desk as he heard footsteps coming his way.

"Walther Roosevelt is on the phone, Your Eminence."

"Thank you," Cardinal Sole said as he picked up the phone.

"Senator Roosevelt, what can I do for you?"

"Well, for one thing, you can start by having a talk with my brother, your bishop. I just got off the phone with him, and in a drunken voice he told me, with your blessing, he is planning on foreclosing the convent property.

Something about a loan they owe the diocese."

"Yes, Senator, your brother just called me about the sisters and some television interview regarding the same matter," also drunk, the cardinal thought.

"I was just getting ready to call you to discuss it."

"Cardinal Sole, I thought we had an understanding. You are well aware of what is buried on that property."

"Yes, I am."

"I think we had an agreement that eventually it would be sent to the Vatican Secret Archives," Walther said.

"Yes, and I am doing everything I can to stall the action on the convent property. However, some here at the Vatican, who have more power than I, are pushing to get this matter over with and may have been speaking with your brother behind my back. They are not so sure your party will win the election and that you will eventually be the next vice president."

"Cardinal, you of all people know how the media or the paparazzi operate. They have to stir up the pot. I assure you I am the nominee, and I will be the next vice president. Tell these men to cool their heels. Now is not the time for this and certainly not anything as public as closing down a convent of nuns. Let me say this one more time. You will have your prize for the Vatican archives, but you must be patient and wait until I am in office. I think we can both agree that neither of us, meaning the U.S. Government or the Vatican, would want to see this played out in the news. Talk to my brother and put a stop to this foreclosure."

"I will call him today, Senator."

"No, I think you should call him right now, Cardinal. You see, if this is not handled today, and you don't back off this foreclosure of the convent and using my brother to get your hands on your prize, those banking problems of yours are going to get mighty serious. *Capiche?*"

"I understand. I will take care of the matter immediately."

Cardinal Sole stared at the phone for the longest time and then looked up at the pope who was walking into his office.

"Everything okay, Cardinal Sole?"

"Yes, Your Holiness. Nothing I can't handle."

23

Charlie, Ernie, and Rodeo were sitting on the top deck of Ernie's houseboat. It was a chilly day for Florida, but the sun felt good. Rodeo had just arrived. They were quiet, sipping their drinks, bourbon over ice.

"Does Velma know you're back," Ernie asked Rodeo.

"No, I was only able to slip away for a short time, just for this meeting, and then I'll be gone again until the mission is complete."

Ernie had called Rodeo and Charlie and asked for a meeting. He had not given a reason, so both men were quiet, waiting for Ernie, who was standing with his back to them and looking out over the water. He looked at his glass of bourbon, raised it, downed it, and then turned and came back. He sat down across from the two men he had known for many years.

"I have information that MC and Velma are mixed up in something very dangerous," Ernie said. "The reason I called you both here today is because I am worried for their safety."

"Why am I not surprised?" Rodeo said as he looked over at Charlie who just shook his head.

"Déjà vu," Charlie said as he took a sip of the bourbon. The three of them had been down this road before with MC and Velma.

"So, tell us, what is it this time?" Rodeo asked Ernie.

"It started with an envelope MC was given by Jennifer Stone. You remember Jennifer Stone?" Ernie asked.

"Oh yes, from past escapades," Rodeo said.

"Jennifer was once married to a man by the name of Harry Stone who had also been a client of yours, Charlie."

"Had been?" Rodeo asked with a raised eyebrow.

Charlie nodded, "He was shot and killed in Miami a couple of weeks ago."

"When he was married to Jennifer, he told me that, in the event of his death, she would deliver an envelope to me with some instructions. He never mentioned it again. After they had divorced, Jennifer became MC's client. Jennifer gave that envelope to MC to deliver to me."

"What was in it?" Rodeo asked. "I'm getting the feeling it had nothing to do with taxes or accounting."

"The envelope contained a piece of paper that showed a puzzle, a crossword puzzle of sorts. That puzzle clearly showed two numbers, which are the latitude and longitude of Key West. It also had an imprint of something that looked like the Mona Lisa," Ernie said.

"Only she was wearing a nun's habit," Charlie said.

"A nun's habit? What does this have to do with MC and my Velma? Are you telling me it's related to whoever killed Harry Stone?" Rodeo asked both men.

"A couple of days ago Charlie and MC were at the bar, and Jennifer showed up with another envelope left behind by Harry Stone. This one contained a copy of an old treasure map, which had been handed down to Harry from his grandfather, Grover P. Stone. His grandfather had left his mansion and land it sits on to the Sisters of Saint Anthony. He is also buried on that land in what is now the convent cemetery," Ernie said.

"Another envelope with a treasure map," Rodeo said rolling his eyes. Both men watched Rodeo stand, all six-feet-plus of him, bend over to a flat back, and then slowly curl straight up, shrug his shoulders, and sit back down finishing with some deep breaths.

Charlie and Ernie stared at him.

"Yoga," Rodeo said as he sat back down.

"It calms my mind and keeps my back strong. I've taken it up since Velma and I got back together. You might try it, Charlie."

"I'll look into it," Charlie said.

"I promised Jennifer I would look into the matter and see if the contents of the envelope and the treasure map were tied together," Ernie said.

"Of course, you did," Rodeo chuckled. "You'd jump off a cliff if that woman asked you to."

Ernie ignored the comment and continued, "Harry Stone was a hedge fund manager. When I first started looking into it, I found out that he also fancied himself a deal maker and a risk taker. His client list included some extremely dangerous men. The only thing he appeared to be afraid of was the IRS, which is why he wanted Charlie as his CPA," Ernie said with a nod toward Charlie.

"When I first met him, he walked into my office and told me he needed a CPA who knew how to deal with the IRS. Like many of my clients, he came to me because of my IRS background and told me that he specifically wanted to avoid trouble with the IRS. Everything else he would handle. I told him I would agree to prepare his tax return, but it had to be clean. Something I tell all my clients when I first meet them. I knew who Harry Stone was just like everybody else did in the town of Fish Camp. That was the basis of our relationship. As his CPA, I oversaw the preparation of his tax returns and let's just say that he paid a lot in taxes for that representation," Charlie said looking back at Ernie who picked up the narrative again.

"I talked to the detective in Miami who was investigating his death. He told me that the evidence pointed towards a professional hit by an unhappy client. An old friend dropped by the bar, and I mentioned the matter to him. He is retired like me, but in the past, he had also been a confidential informant of mine. He did some checking and got back to me with something very interesting. He said there was chatter going around that Harry Stone may have been killed because of something his grandfather had found a long time ago on land that is now part of the naval air station in the Keys," Ernie said.

"His grandfather, the one who passed down the treasure map to Harry and is buried in the convent cemetery?" Rodeo asked.

"Yes, his grandfather, Grover P. Stone or as he was known, Pirate Pete," Ernie said.

"Yeah, Pirate Pete," Rodeo said with a little nod of his head.

"Now we have two envelopes, one with a mysterious matrix and another with a treasure map. Both delivered by the beautiful Jennifer Stone who makes Ernie's eyes go crosswise and other body parts go haywire. It involves her ex, Harry Stone, who appears to have been killed by some unhappy investors. To complicate matters, the map deals with something Pirate Pete, his grandfather, found on what is now a government installation located in the Keys. So again, what does this have to do with my Velma? I'm afraid to ask. And MC?" Rodeo said looking at Charlie.

"You are familiar with the bar, Buried Money, in Key West?"

"Yes, I've been there," Rodeo said.

"As I recall it's not too far from the naval air station."

"Apparently, Harry's grandfather aka Pirate Pete owned it at one time. The story goes that one day he walked into the bar and told everyone he was retiring. That was the last day he set foot in the bar. He moved to Fish Camp, built a mansion, and left everything to the Sisters of Saint Anthony when he died."

"This scenario has gotten complicated. According to my source, it also involves Walther Roosevelt," Ernie said.

"Walther Roosevelt?" both Charlie and Rodeo said in unison.

"The three of us have seen firsthand how Walther Roosevelt's idealistic beliefs and ambitions cloud his judgment," Ernie said.

"I have solid intelligence that indicates Walther Roosevelt will be his party's nominee for vice president."

"Don't tell me MC and Velma are involved in something to do with Walther Roosevelt and his nomination?"

"I'm afraid so," Ernie said.

"Dang," Charlie said.

"MC and Velma not only stand squarely in the cross hairs of Walther becoming the next vice president of the United States, but it also involves a scandal that could bring down the pope of the Catholic Church," Ernie said.

"And this all ties into the envelopes and some old treasure map?" Rodeo asked incredulously.

"I don't get it," Charlie said.

"How does all this tie into this envelope left for me by Harry Stone?"

"Harry Stone and his grandfather were descendants of the pirate Blackbeard who seems to have buried his treasure all over Florida. When Pirate Pete was a young man, his father passed on the treasure map. The map gave him a pretty good idea where some of the treasure was buried, so he headed to Key West. Around the time of World War I, the year-round good weather and the strategic location of Key West led the Navy to a decision to establish a naval air station and a submarine base in Key West in the summer of 1917. Ground was being broken for construction of the naval air station, and Pirate Pete got himself a job on the construction projects. It gave him access to the area. While he was employed on those projects, he uncovered some of his ancestor's treasure. He stayed in Key West and bought the bar Buried Money because he figured there was more treasure to be found. The last time he went treasure hunting he found something else. Shortly after that, he sold the bar and moved to Fish Camp and built his home and retired."

"He found something else?" Charlie asked.

Ernie turned to face both Charlie and Rodeo and very quietly said, "According to my source who owed me a few favors, besides a valuable treasure, he may have found the remains of a being not of this earth," Ernie said.

"Are you saying Pirate Pete, Harry's grandfather, uncovered an alien?" Rodeo asked shaking his head.

"If not an alien, then something that would suggest aliens have visited the earth. And my source told me that somewhere on the property he left to the sisters are the unearthly remains he found."

"MC and Velma are heading right into the path of a CAT 5, and it may be up to us to keep them out of harm's way," Ernie said to the two men who were sitting there stunned.

"Walther Roosevelt is aware of what is buried on the convent property and has known it for a long time. He is, after all, the head of congressional and senate committees overseeing counterterrorism activity. He has also worked out a deal with the Vatican through a Cardinal Sole. He has offered them what is buried on the property for the Secret Vatican Archives. The cardinal is their librarian, and it would be a feather in his red cap. The Catholic Church has long been interested in alien life, and if there is proof, the Vatican will want it placed in the Secret Vatican Archives," Ernie paused briefly.

"The cardinal has some shady dealings with the Vatican Bank, Walther is aware of that and is using it to keep the cardinal in line. This would take care of the sleeping dragon for the U.S. government.

The three of us need to keep surveillance on MC and Velma until I find this alien," Ernie said.

"How do you plan to do that?" Charlie asked.

"Through an old friend who has a research vessel," Ernie said to Charlie with a wink.

"Walther will have no choice but to back off. He can't let the cat out of that bag, easy, breezy."

"Who are we working for Ernie?" Rodeo now asked.

"Let's just say someone who would like to win this next election and stay in office. We'll leave it at that."

Rodeo looked at Ernie, over at Charlie and then back at Ernie.

"I need another drink. Nothing is ever easy, breezy where MC and Velma are concerned. We have all come to learn that."

"Amen, brother, amen," Charlie said as he downed a double shot.

24

MC was flipping through the channels on her TV and froze when she saw Aunt Sophia on the local 24-hour cable news channel. She thought she had landed on the public access TV channel, but double-checked and confirmed that it was not public access. It looked like the cable news channel was interviewing Aunt Sophia, and right next to her sat Aunt Anna.

"So, do you have any interesting interviews coming up on Montage?" the cable news host asked Aunt Sophia. MC got closer to her TV as if it was going to make a difference.

MC watched as the camera focused on her two aunts as the interview came to an end. They were smiling into the camera and were dressed in their Sunday going to church power outfits, which made them look very sympathetic because they looked like everyone's grandmother.

"As a matter of fact, we recently sat down with Sister Hildegard, the Mother Superior of the Sisters of Saint Anthony. The Vatican has decided to audit Catholic nuns in the U.S."

"Audit, you mean like the IRS? Are they actually looking at their books and records?"

"Not exactly, but along the same lines," Aunt Sophia responded.

"Crap," MC said as she sat down on the edge of her couch and watched with anticipation.

"They are calling them feisty nuns," Aunt Anna offered up.

"Feisty nuns?" The cable news reporter asked with a chuckle.

"The Vatican claims some of the sisters have serious doctrinal problems," Aunt Sophia said while MC watched her aunt speak straight into the camera without flinching. Aunt Anna nodded her head and smiled into the camera as Aunt Sophia maintained her poker face.

"Serious doctrinal problems?" the cable news reporter said.

"I grew up in a Catholic household and, although the sisters at my grade school were intimidating, they had a strong influence on my making it through school while staying out of trouble. Why would the Vatican be concerned about nuns?"

"Well, that is something you might want to ask Bishop Michael Roosevelt," Aunt Anna responded before Aunt Sophia had a chance to answer. The camera panned to Aunt Sophia who now smiled into the camera. Then she gave her sister a look MC knew as the evil eye.

"It's my understanding, after talking with Sister Hildegard, that the nuns are being reprimanded because they take on social causes, which could be viewed as challenging the all-male leadership of the church," Aunt Sophia said taking back control of the interview.

"Like what?" the cable reporter asked.

"Well, a number of hot button topics including the lack leadership roles for women in the church," Aunt Sophia said.

"Holy crap," I now said out loud. What has gotten into Aunt Sophia? Did Sister Hildegard give her the green light to air the interview?

"We look forward to airing our interview with Sister Hildegard sometime in the near future on our public access show, *Montage*," Aunt Sophia responded.

MC watched as the camera focused up close on Aunt Sophia.

"Viewers, don't forget your sisters. They have done, and still do, remarkable work. We'll be doing a fundraiser down at the public access studio to help the sisters. We'd like everyone to join us."

"Thank you, Sophia and thank you, Anna. We look forward to watching that interview and finding out more about that fundraiser for the sisters. We will pass along the date and information for our viewers."

"There you have it, a crackdown by the Vatican on Catholic nuns. The Vatican claims nuns have become too feisty for the all-male leadership of the Catholic Church."

I immediately grabbed my cell and called Aunt Sophia only to get her voicemail.

"Crap and double dang," I said out loud.

I saw that I had a message on my phone. It was my Aunt Anna reminding me that tonight was the birthday celebration for Aunt Sophia. I grabbed my purse and cell and hopped into my car. I sped all the way to the public access TV station.

I made my way across the campus and through hordes of students heading to the university's student center.

"Great," I said to myself. The public access TV studio was in a small building close to the student center. Finally, I made it to the front door of the public access TV studio and ran head on into Molly and Harold, members of my aunts' show crew.

"MC, we're so glad you could make it. Your Aunt Sophia will be so surprised," Molly said. Molly at eighty-three still looked and moved like the dancer she had been. Her red hair, cut short with bangs, framed her blue eyes as they looked out from between her freckles.

"Yes, she should be here any minute. Might have got tied up in the big concert traffic on campus," Harold said.

Standing next to Molly was her shadow, Harold. Besides being smitten with Molly, he was a true gentleman in every sense of the word. Harold was eighty-six, trim, sharply dressed, and retired military.

Before I knew it, I heard a familiar voice and was wrapped up in a huge hug. It was Velma's Aunt Sadie. I smiled and returned the hug.

"You look amazing," I said to Aunt Sadie who smiled from ear to ear and strutted across the lobby of the studio.

"Down 50 pounds," she said. "I owe it all to Bruce who introduced me to Zumba. There are always a lot of good looking men at Zumba, and I want to make sure they can see my hips moving," she said with a wicked grin on her face.

Aunt Sadie took me by the hand, and we walked into Studio A, where Montage was filmed and waiting for my Aunt Sophia was a huge cake with a candle on top that looked like a firecracker.

I saw a lot of people I recognized from the years when my mother was the driving force behind the TV show. Many of them came up to me and told me how much they loved her and missed her, and how much I looked like her. At that moment, I felt a wave of love in the room, and for a second I looked around because I thought for sure I caught her belly laugh coming from the other side of the room.

"I miss you, Mom," I whispered and felt her spirit nearby as a roar of applause took place, and I turned to see my Aunts Sophia and Anna entering the room.

Their eyes rested on me, their faces lit up, and at that moment I was so glad I was there for my Aunt Sophia. They came over and gave me hugs, then Aunt Sophia took my hand and led me around the room introducing me to everyone, just as my mother would have done in her place.

Music came on, and the party rolled on with cake and ice cream and singing *Happy Birthday*. Although I wanted to take my Aunt Sophia aside, but now was not the moment to do so. My Aunt Sophia guessed as much, and after the song was over, she led me over to the side of the room.

"I guess you saw the interview on cable news today," she said.

"Yes, I did. I thought I was catching an airing of *Montage*, but there was both you and Aunt Anna. What's next? *Sixty Minutes*?"

She looked at me, and then gave me a smile with a nod of her eyebrows.

"It all happened very quickly. Sister Hildegard called me today to talk about the audit and then the possibility of a foreclosure of the convent property. She told me it gave her more courage to stand up to the church audit. She also told me she was just about ready to give me the green light to air the interview. We're going to get together soon and pick a date," she said.

"We just happened to be down at the cable station and saw Johnnie, so stopped to say hello."

"Johnnie?" I said.

"Yes, the news reporter that interviewed me today. He interned on *Montage* when he was a college student."

"Oh, I see," I said.

"Your Aunt Anna, of course, had to spill the beans about the bishop and the audit of the Sisters of Saint Anthony. Anyway, the next thing I knew he was interviewing us, and it just seemed as if it was meant to happen," Aunt Sophia said.

"Aunt Sophia, I think it was," I said as my Aunt Sophia smiled and gave me a big hug.

"I guess, as you say, it was in the cards."

With that, she grabbed my hand. "Time to dance." The music was starting, and they were playing *Zorba the Greek.*

25

I got up early Monday morning and spent a couple of hours at the courthouse and found no record of any lien being filed by the diocese on the convent property. The document Sister Clarissa had presented to me the other day at lunch had never been recorded either. There was far less legal standing for a foreclosure without a lien on the convent property. Still, it could engage the convent in a legal battle with the bishop and costly legal fees, which could force them to sell the convent property and halt all current projects in their tracks.

Charlie and I met for lunch, and I told him about my morning at the courthouse and about the loan. I pulled out the loan document and asked him to look at it. He took a quick glance and gave it back to me and said, "It's a fake and not a very good one."

"How do you know?"

"Take a look at the bottom of the loan document."

I did. I looked back up at him with an 'Okay I don't see it' look on my face. How is it I can see things no one else can, but sometimes I can't see what's right in front of my nose? I was thinking about the Mona Lisa wearing the nun's habit.

"Look again," he said with his eyes pointing at the lower right-hand corner.

When I looked again, I saw it. There in the corner was a bar code.

"Oh, why didn't I catch that?"

"Too close to the emotional side," Charlie said. "It must mess up that psychic radar of yours. Obviously, they didn't have barcodes back when the bishop is purporting this loan was taken out by the Sisters of Saint Anthony," Charlie said.

"Thank you."

"MC, you need to be very careful," he now said very seriously.

"Why, do you think the bishop is going to excommunicate me? Too late," I said with a chuckle.

Charlie was eyeing me very carefully.

"No, it's not the bishop I'm worried about. It's his brother, Walther, a very influential man becoming more so," he said.

"Walther Roosevelt? I doubt that Senator Roosevelt is going to get involved in this matter. According to the news, he's kind of busy running for vice president."

My psychic radar told me he knew something he wasn't saying.

"What are you getting at, Charlie? Is there something you are not telling me?"

He just looked at me. He started to say something, but I could see in his eyes he thought better not to say.

"Just be careful is all I am saying," Charlie said as he reached across the table and gave my hand a squeeze. "Both you and Velma, that's all."

"You know something you're not telling me. Is Walther Roosevelt tied into this matter with his brother and the nuns?"

Charlie stared at me for a long time and then said,

"Yes, he is, and that is why you need to be careful. I am very serious, MC."

"Does it have something to do with the convent property?" I asked out of nowhere.

"You should talk to Ernie about that, but in the meantime, would you and Velma, please watch your backs?"

After lunch, I headed back to the office where Velma and my client appointments kept me busy for the rest of the afternoon. As we were wrapping up the day, Velma came in, and we finished up some paperwork together, and then I poured us each a glass of wine to relax. I kept thinking about Charlie and our conversation at lunch, and something prompted me to ask Velma about Rodeo.

"Have you heard from Rodeo, recently?"

I could see from her reaction and the look in her eyes that she had not only heard from Rodeo, but she had seen Rodeo, and had some Velma and Rodeo time.

"I saw him last night, but he was just passing through, and he left again early this morning."

"Isn't that a little odd?"

"Yes, it's never happened before, but I was so happy to see him," Velma said.

"Did he say anything about the bishop or his brother, Walther?"

"Yes, he did, just as he was leaving," Velma said.

"What did he say?"

"Just that you and I should be careful where Bishop Michael is concerned and not to forget his brother Walther is a very powerful man. He used a very solemn tone," Velma said.

"Strange," I said. "I had pretty much the same conversation today with Charlie at lunch."

"What do you make of it?" Velma said.

"I don't know, but I think I'll drop in for a drink this evening at the tiki bar and have a talk with Ernie. Charlie suggested I do that."

"Good luck, MC. You know you can't get anything out of Ernie unless he is ready to talk."

I knew she was right about Ernie, and then it came to me. I should talk to Theo and not Ernie. It was as if I was receiving a message from the psychic side of the brain. We finished our wine and closed up the office. I decided to head home instead of going to see Ernie. Something was brewing like a Florida storm, and I could feel it in my bones. The barometer was dropping, and a storm was heading our way.

26

Walther sat while Michael was told by the butler that he had a call from Rome. He watched his brother, and he saw a look of sheer disappointment come over him. When Michael got off the phone and reached for a drink, he knew the time had come to put a stop to his brother's drinking.

He watched as Sister Clarissa got up and took the bottle from his brother. "Thank you," Walther said, and she nodded.

"Sister Clarissa, the visitation with the Sisters of St. Anthony is being…postponed. It seems that the current pope will be stepping down due to health reasons and all visitations are on hold until after the next pope is chosen. If he is liberal and progressive, this whole visitation business may be dropped entirely. You are to return to Rome and await further instructions," Michael said as he finished his drink.

Sister Clarissa smiled benignly and said, "I'll pack and catch the first plane out."

She got up and started to leave the room. Walther followed her out into the hallway.

"Sister Clarissa, I'd like to ask you to stay on a little longer," he said. "You will receive a call from your superiors in Rome shortly allowing an extension of your stay."

"I don't understand," Sister Clarissa said.

"Please sit down," he said. He led her to a small bench. "You are no doubt aware that my brother has a problem with his drinking. He needs to stop. Sister, I am about to accept the nomination for the vice president of the United States. I need my brother sober."

"I see," she said.

"In return for your help, I am certain I can find you a position here in the United States, which will be attractive to you. You might consider this instead of returning to Rome and all those stuffy men," he said as if he was making a joke, but he was confident Sister Clarissa got the message.

Sister Clarissa looked at Walther and then said,

"What do you need from me?"

Walther smiled at her.

"I need you to be my eyes and ears while he undergoes rehab. I have arranged for that to take place here in his beautiful home."

She looked thoughtfully at the senator and then said, "Fine, consider it done, and we will discuss that other position now."

Walther remained quiet while looking at her directly. "What did you have in mind?"

"I would like a position in your administration. A newly created position, we'll give it a title later. I will be the liaison between your administration and the Curia in Rome."

Walther considered her carefully and then nodded his head, "That can be done."

"Thank you. Religious women like me cannot compete with those *stuffy* men in Rome that make up the Catholic Church leadership. I've gone as far as I can in my current—capacity. This will do just fine, and I promise you I will see to it that your brother stops drinking. I will make it my personal mission for as long as you see fit."

"Very well, Sister Clarissa, consider it done."

Walther watched as she got up and walked down the hall. He returned to his brother.

"Michael, you are going to stop drinking today. I have asked Sister Clarissa to stay on to oversee your rehab. I am sending you a team of experts that will be here later today. They and Sister Clarissa will be in charge of your rehab. Once and for all, Michael, you must stop drinking."

"Don't worry, good brother, I will stop drinking. I will not be an embarrassment to you as the next vice president of the United States. Unfortunately, with a new pope, I can see that any chance of my advancement in the church probably has gone right out the window."

"Not necessarily. As vice president, I will look into a new post of duty for you in the bigger and more significant pond of Washington. I am confident that—if you become and remain sober—when the time comes, it will lead to your appointment as a cardinal, which would give you more leverage and power."

Walther stepped closer to his brother and spoke directly into his ear, "But this can only happen if you do not have another drop of booze for the rest of your life."

"Well, it might work out if I can have you close to me and Sister Clarissa keeping an eye on me," Michael said.

Walther grabbed his brother by his shirt collar, pulled him right out of his seat, got right into his face and said, "Listen very carefully to what I am about to say, Michael, because I am not going to repeat it. If you fall off the wagon, I will see to it that you rot in a black site. You will never, ever see the light of day." With that, he shoved him back into his chair.

"I'd also suggest you move out of these fancy trappings into something more modest,"

Walther said as he walked out of the room. "Mother of God, Michael, this place is larger than the White House."

27

Velma poked her head into my office and said, "You have a visitor." I looked up and there, in the doorway, stood Theo, the last person on earth I thought I would see at that moment. Needless to say, I was speechless. I had spent most of the day while meeting with clients thinking about picking up the phone and calling him, for more reasons than one, and now it looked like the call wouldn't be necessary.

"Hello, Mary Catherine," he said casually as he stepped into my office and I knew, with no help from the psychic side of my brain, right back into my life. I watched as he sat down, and as Velma, with a smile and a wink, closed the door while saying she was leaving early for the day.

"Hello, Theo," I said. "Long time, no see."

He sat there smiling his Theo smile, which always melted me like a slab of butter on a flaky, hot biscuit. I watched as he got up, walked around my desk to my back window and looked out at the docks.

"Hello, Izzy," he said.

I looked up and could see Izzy on the window ledge outside peering in at Theo. I sat there while Theo and Izzy reconnected. Like everyone else, Theo was fond of Izzy.

I stood and walked over, and when Izzy saw me, he jumped off the window ledge. I looked out the window, and across the canal, I saw the Mary Catherine.

"You're docked behind my office?"

"Yes," he said as he took me in his arms and kissed me as if he had been doing it for a thousand years. I guess you could say that sealed the deal.

"Just for a few days, but I'm flexible. I might even get a slip over at Ernie and Charlie's marina and stay a bit longer," he said as he released me from his arms.

I walked back to my desk and sat, mentally seeking the protection of my office desk as if sitting behind it would protect me from letting go of all that control.

"Do Aunt Sophia and Aunt Anna know you are here?"

"Yes, I happened to run into them and joined them for lunch. I also had the pleasure of meeting two delightful nuns, Sister Hildegard and Sister Matilda," he said with a twinkle in his eye and took a seat across from me. Great, I thought, they probably have joined the Theo fan club along with my two aunts.

"We had a very stimulating conversation, and then the two sisters insisted on taking me back to the convent where they showed me all around. Sister Matilda and I had quite a discussion about the history of the property. She is quite the history buff when it comes to treasure."

"Yes, she is, and so, during your visit, did the conversation of treasure hunting come up?"

"Yes, it did. Seems like they have been busy bees, those nuns. Then they asked me to do something odd. There was one place they wanted to check and needed help getting to it. They needed some muscle was how Sister Hildegard put it. I did, and then I took the liberty of calling Ernie.

"Why?"

"Because he works for the government."

"Yes, I'm aware of that," I said.

"What are you trying to tell me?" I continued. "Did you find something? Is the government involved? I was actually going to call you. Where did they need help to look?" I asked as I reached down and pulled out the piece of paper that had started all this. Something was telling me to take another look at the Mona Lisa.

As I looked, I saw it. "Good grief, how did I miss that?"

The Mona Lisa in the nun's habit was standing in front of a credenza.

"Why had I not seen that before?" I said to Theo, and as I did I recalled Charlie's words,

"Too close to the emotional side."

"You found something behind the credenza in their bomb shelter," I said.

"You know, Mary Catherine, you really are psychic, just like your mother used to tell me," Theo said with a look of amazement on his face.

"Wow," I said looking at the Mona Lisa, and when I looked up, I was looking into his dark Greek eyes. He leaned over my desk, pulled me up, and gave me a long and passionate kiss, which literally took my breath away. When he let me go, I moved my chair a few inches back from my desk, my safe harbor where I was in control, or at least I thought so—until this moment. As he stood there with those Greek eyes staring intently at me, I anxiously decided I better keep some conversation going.

"Yeah, what else did my mother tell you? You were her favorite, you know."

"Just that one day you would wake up, and we would be together again."

He stood and walked back over to the window, looked out at the canal, and as he did so he said,

"When I helped move that credenza, we did find something had been hidden behind it."

"Treasure?" I asked.

"Yes, treasure and—something else, which is why I called Ernie back," Theo said still standing by the window.

"Called Ernie back?"

"That is why I am here. Ernie actually called me first and asked me to pay a visit to the sisters at the convent. He told me they were having lunch with your aunts and told me where to find them. It was easy since they invited me back to the convent. If I didn't know better, I would say those two nuns are psychic."

"So, spook Ernie set this up, and behind the credenza sat Pirate Pete's treasure. Well, you made their day. They will be forever grateful for your help Theo, you have no idea," I said thinking their financial woes should be over.

"Tell me why Ernie called you. Why would the government be interested in treasure? It's not on government property," I said from the psychic part of my brain.

"The government doesn't care about the treasure. What they do care about is the government property that was also hidden by Pirate Pete behind his credenza with that treasure a long time ago. Harry Stone told me an important artifact was part of the treasure. That is why I agreed to help him. I had no idea what it was until I moved the credenza, and found it," he said.

"After finding the treasure and the artifact, Sister Hildegard and Sister Matilda and I talked for a long time. The Sisters gave me the artifact, with the agreement that I would return it to the sea, so it can be at peace."

"Okay, Theo. This other thing? This artifact? What the hell is it? An alien?" I said that as if it had come to me from some forgotten memory. He just looked at me for the longest time, and then I knew exactly why.

"Are you freaking kidding me?"

"No, I'm not. The sisters said you were to join me, and in doing so, things would come full circle. You and I are going to return it to the sea where it was found by Pirate Pete, a long time ago. Only we are going to make sure it is buried much deeper and never found again. We will head east almost to Freeport.

I reached down into my purse, pulled out the copy of the map, and we both looked at it.

"So then, what was this all about?"

"The map shows a large X over what is now the Naval Air Station in Key West. It also stretches out to the body of water, which is part of the National Marine Sanctuary," he said pointing to the X, and as he did, I saw what he was describing.

"Sister Matilda, talking today about the history of the property, figured out that right about the time Pirate Pete came to Fish Camp to retire, a small hurricane had made landfall near Key West. It must have disturbed the location where the alien had been buried as well as treasure," he said.

"She said the puzzle and the Mona Lisa were clues as to the treasure that was hidden on convent property. His grandfather had passed it on to Harry along with the treasure map."

"So, this treasure map points to a treasure hidden in Key West in the area around the Naval Air Station and the National Marine Sanctuary," I said.

"Yes," he said.

"Somehow, and for reasons unknown, we have all been drawn into this," Theo said. "Sister Hildegard said it was God's will."

"So, what else did Ernie say when you called him. Did he know who killed Harry Stone?"

"He thinks it was some very unhappy investors. He agreed to give us a head start. Let's go."

"Now?"

"We don't have much time. The engines are running on the Mary Catherine. I'll see you on the Mary Catherine." He headed right out the door.

And so, shortly after that, I followed. I looked back at my office, and then I walked straight out the front door. As I did, I just knew I was not coming back to this life. I walked out of my office and right into the next life.

28

And so, that night, under the moonlight, Theo piloted the Mary Catherine east in the direction of Freeport, and I was by his side.

"When the sun rises I will take the one-man submarine and return this being to the sea." We were the only two on the ship, but I looked around anyway to make sure no one was listening.

"Wait a minute. I'm going to wait here while you dive deep with a one-man submarine?"

"No, you won't just be waiting. You'll need to keep an eye out. It should take me about an hour. Use Gertrude if you need to contact me."

"Gertrude, who's Gertrude and keep an eye out for what? The Coast Guard?"

"Gertrude is that yellow handset just inside the cabin there. I don't have time to explain it now, but if you pick the handset and talk, I will be able to hear you and talk back. As for what you are looking out for, I wish it was the Coast Guard, they would not be a problem for me. No, I am concerned with probable government operatives. Ernie said they would be coming once they figured out the alien had been found. The convent has probably been under satellite surveillance, and Walther Roosevelt would be notified immediately of any suspicious activity."

I got a shiver up my spine and said, "Theo, this is why I should have stayed on land, safe and sound."

"Yes, safe and sound, and in control. But sometimes, Mary Catherine, you need to just believe that when the time comes you will know what to do, and you will do the right thing."

"What if I screw up? What if you run into trouble in that submarine and I can't help you?"

"We've gone over the Mayday procedures," he said. "You know what to do and how to use the radio. Remember that is the red handset near the wheel."

"But what if Walther Roosevelt's men show up and board us?"

"What should you do, my Mary Catherine? That's when you listen to your inner voice. It will tell you what to do; you just do it and expect the best. Always remember, I love you, even if you screw up."

With that, he handed me a gun. "Just in case, I know you know how to use this," he said as he gave me one of those kisses that told me I could do anything with this man next to me.

"Don't worry, you will be just fine. Trust me. Plus, you will have some help," Theo said and nodded in the direction behind me.

"Help?" I said as I turned around and let out a high pitched "yikes" because there stood Izzy. "What are you doing here?" I said as he made his way to right under my feet and looked up at me attempting to draw on his inner cuteness.

"It's not going to work," I said looking down at Izzy. He agreed and made his way over next to Theo.

"How did he get here?" I asked as I looked over at Theo and Izzy, both were now quiet and innocent looking. Theo looked down at Izzy, who looked up at Theo, and then Theo looked at me and shrugged his shoulders.

"Yeah, right," I said looking at Izzy who stood his ground next to Theo.

"I told Ernie to let Velma know so she wouldn't worry," Theo said while we both watched Izzy take off and disappear.

"You can run, but you can't hide, Izzy," I said, and then I could have sworn I heard, "You'll have to catch me first," followed by laughing.

Was that Izzy? Are you talking to me?

"Did you hear that?" I asked Theo.

"Hear what?" Theo replied as he took me into his arms and kissed me and held me pressed close to him. "Your heart beating?" Soon after that, I forgot about Izzy.

In the early dawn, I watched as Theo prepared his one-man submarine, and then he brought up a sealed container and a small urn. Right behind him followed Izzy. We were in deep water, not too far from Freeport and the devil's triangle.

As the sun rose, Theo said a prayer in Greek, and I recited the 23rd Psalm, as Izzy stood close by. Theo then placed the urn in the sealed container for its return to the sea. We both then watched as Izzy placed his little iguana paw on the container, his way of paying his respects to another one of God's creatures.

"Some things should be left alone," Theo said to me. "They should be in their natural setting."

"If that is the case, it should be returned to its home planet or wherever it came from," I said.

"I have a feeling it will, one day."

"Is that what Sister Hildegard told you?"

"No, a strange dream I had last night. A gypsy came to me and told me."

"Was her name Pythia?"

He looked at me. "You are psychic."

"Really, was it Pythia? An old gypsy woman that looks like a character out of *Game of Thrones*?"

He smiled at me broadly.

"You're playing with me?"

"No. It was something inside of me, my inner voice." I looked at Theo wondering if he had some psychic intuition of his own. He stared at me and then looked far out to sea.

"I did have a dream not too long ago, though. It was your mother. She said she had a message for you that she never got to tell you. She told me to tell you the time was now for you to follow your heart," and with that, he gave me another long kiss, and I knew in my inner voice it was time to follow him for the rest of my life.

Izzy and I watched as the one-man submarine submerged, and then we found ourselves alone on the Mary Catherine. I became increasingly anxious, almost claustrophobic.

"Where is he, Izzy?" I said, and as I did so, Izzy disappeared.

"Thanks, some pal you are," I muttered mentally going over how to make a mayday call on the radio.

I stood there with my eyes fixed on the intended rendezvous spot waiting for Theo's return, so I didn't hear anyone board the Mary Catherine until it was too late.

Suddenly, standing in front of me were two men, and I knew they were not government operatives. I knew they were pirates. They came with their guns.

"Ms. Mahoney, we were clients of Harry Stone, and we are here to collect on a bad investment that Mr. Stone made, unfortunately, on our behalf. As soon as your boyfriend returns, we will take this lovely vessel, which bears your name, and head back to the Keys to go on a little treasure hunt. Before Mr. Stone met his unfortunate death, he told us of a map which pinpoints the location of buried treasure. We found a copy of that old treasure map in his condo. This vessel, we are sure, is well equipped for a treasure hunt."

I had placed the gun Theo gave me under a chair cushion, and I was contemplating whether I should grab it when I heard a voice. That's when I saw Izzy under the chair, and I realized the voice I heard was Izzy.

"Don't grab that gun unless you want to get killed, sister," Izzy said, sounding a lot like a gangster from an old movie.

"Keep calm," Izzy continued as I looked at the two pirates who were looking out to sea. They had not seen Izzy and clearly could not hear him either; only I could. My psychic genes were growing stronger with the increased danger.

The water started to bubble and up came the one-man submarine. The two pirates pointed their gun at me while we watched it dock and Theo emerge. He started to say something, but then his words went silent as he looked at the two men and the guns pointed at me. I looked around, and Izzy was gone.

"Get up here, Captain, we have some treasure to find, and we don't have much time."

Theo came over and stood next to me, and then we both looked at the two men with guns pointed at us, and without flinching, we saw two more pirates coming on board. By the looks of their camouflage, they were the government operatives.

Theo and I watched as they came up behind the two pirates. When one of the pirates turned around and saw the new guys, he scooted over, grabbed me, and pulled me away from Theo.

"Hold it right there," he said as I felt the barrel of his weapon right under my chin.

Out of the corner of my eye and in my peripheral vision I could see Izzy, down by the pirate's ankle.

"Don't move, sister," Izzy said to me, and then I heard a loud scream from the pirate as he looked down to see Izzy taking a bite out of his ankle, probably his Achilles tendon. He screamed as he dropped to the ground, but still held onto his gun and aimed it at the government operatives.

Shots rang out. Izzy scrambled. Theo grabbed me, and the two of us ducked behind the one-man submarine. In a second, it was all over.

"We have orders to take a certain artifact with us. You will need to get it," the leader of the group said as we watched more men appear and very quickly remove the bodies of the two pirates. Once again Izzy was nowhere to be found.

"That's not going to happen," Theo said.

"Sir, we don't have time to argue. Please take the submarine and return with the artifact."

"I can't," Theo said.

The leader pulled out a cell and made a call. Then he paused and handed the cell to me.

"Someone wishes to speak to you, ma'am."

I took the cell and placed it next to my ear, and as I did so, Izzy appeared and took his place next to Theo.

"MC, this is Senator Walther Roosevelt. I think you and your friend Theo have some government property that needs to be turned over to the two men standing in front of you."

I looked down at Izzy, and I could hear him say, "No way, brother. E.T. is going nowhere near you." I nodded at Izzy.

"That is not possible, Senator Roosevelt," I said as I heard a big sigh on the other end.

"Why not?" he asked.

"You remember all those years ago, a rumor circulating that you were using the IRS to harass your political opponents."

"Well, MC, what I recall, all those years ago, is the end of your government employment. This is more serious. You wouldn't want anything happening to Theo now, would you?"

I looked down at Izzy and heard him say, "He's never been bitten by an iguana, has he?" I smiled at Izzy and then at Theo who was giving me a '*what's going on?*' look.

"Nothing is going to happen to anyone today, Senator Roosevelt. I have been told, by a reliable source, that they possess some *interesting* documents. Documents that you would not want to see the light of day."

"And MC, how do I know you are not bluffing?"

"Call this number, and it will be confirmed."

There was nothing but silence on the other end after I gave him the number. I handed the cell back to the leader. He listened for a moment and then put the cell back in his vest pocket.

We all waited and then we watched as the leader put the cell next to his ear and then ended the conversation once again.

"Well, ma'am and sir. It seems that we will be leaving now." As they returned to the sea, the two soldiers saluted Izzy and said, "Good job today, little guy." Izzy stood as tall and as best as an iguana could, and he returned their salute. "Amazing," the soldiers said to each other.

Later that evening, Theo and I watched the setting sun as we drank a toast to the beautiful sunset and to karma. Izzy sat nearby and snored quietly.

"What was at the end of that telephone number Mary Catherine?"

"Our dear friend Ernie. The number I gave Walther Roosevelt was Ernie's. He told me it was my get out of jail free card. That he would take care of the problem, whatever it was if he got the call."

"Did he say how?"

"Nope, only that if he told me he would have to shoot me and I believed him."

"My, oh, my, Mary Catherine," and with that, he reached over and gave me what my mother would have called a smooch and then took my hand and led me below saying, "Have I ever showed you around your namesake?"

29

And so, I opened that big fat appointment book called life and found the appointment I had been putting off for a long, long time. I showed up and kept that appointment with Theo on that eventful day. I would not cancel it or put it off anymore. I knew in doing so I was not going back to the comfort and safety of my tax office. I was leaving the world of order and structure where financial statements were black and white and always balanced.

Instead, I took a leap of faith, said a prayer to Saint Anthony, jumped off the dock and landed in a new life. It wasn't black and white, but brilliant color and it wasn't a life of order and structure.

Every day has become a different adventure. I knew I would spend the rest of my days on the Mary Catherine and wherever else Theo would lead us. I relinquished the control and structure and predictable order in my life, and as I did, I felt a great relief in letting it go. I felt free, and I wondered what took me so long.

Theo and I returned to Fish Camp for the wedding of Velma and Rodeo. The wedding was held at the Baptist Church where Bessie, Velma's mother, ruled the roost. It was one grand party with the best music, country, blues, rock and roll, and a little gospel. The coolest thing was that the wedding took place on the birthday of their twin girls, who walked down the aisle as beautiful bridesmaids. Ernie was best man, and it was also fitting that he gave away the bride. Charlie and Theo were part of the wedding, and it was my honor to be Velma's matron of honor. My aunts were there along with Sister Hildegard and Sister Matilda. Izzy stood up front right next to Velma as she and Rodeo exchanged vows.

The next day the same wedding party arrived on Ernie's houseboat where Theo and I renewed our vows. Sister Hildegard officiated, and my aunts Sophia and Anna brought plenty of Greek food and drink. We danced into the night and finished the evening with a rousing rendition of Zorba the Greek, led by Bruce.

"Your mother is here," Aunt Sophia whispered to me, and out of the corner of my psychic eye, I was sure I caught a glimpse of her dancing and laughing and smiling at me.

Later that year Jennifer and Joe had an announcement of their own. They had just returned from Las Vegas where they had been married, and they would be parents in the New Year. Jennifer shared with me that Joe had come around and was on board with the idea that motherhood would not mean giving up her dream of becoming a country singer.

"Joe was even making arrangements for a nursery at the Full Moon Saloon."

The bishop sold his mansion and moved into a more modest home. The last I heard, he was joining his brother, Senator Roosevelt, and moving to D.C. We heard Sister Clarissa was also heading to D.C. She had been given an influential job on the staff of Senator

Roosevelt, who had bounced back after the election and the defeat of his party. The news was that he still on the fast track in his party to be considered for the presidency. Well, the two of them will do very well in a city of ambitious souls.

The news also reported that the Sisters of Saint Anthony had come into a large sum of money, a donation, and by all accounts were putting it to good use. Pope Benny stepped down amidst the scandal of the Vatican Bank.

Cardinal Sole emerged unscathed, but no longer had the same power as Sister Hildegard had prayed. A new pope, a more progressive pope, had been chosen.

We heard from Sister Hildegard and Sister Matilda that the new pope, who they called Pope Frankie, was planning a trip to the U.S. and the Sisters of Saint Anthony had been invited to meet him.

I sold my tax and accounting practice to Charlie. He and Velma get along just fine. He lets her run the practice, which she does so well, allowing him time in the off-season for the real love of his life, fishing. He gave me one last kiss the day we signed the contract and said, "I will always love you, MC. I wish you only the best."

Aunt Sophia, Aunt Anna, and I Skype daily, which keeps me up to date on all the news on the home front. They are both quite busy down at the public access studio, and now Aunt Sophia has a spot on the local cable news program with her friend, Johnnie. They finally did air the interview with Sister Hildegard on their public access show *Montage*. It went viral and became known everywhere as the *Feisty Nuns Interview*. Sister Hildegard told my two aunts that the interview was part of the reason Pope Frankie wanted to meet them on his trip to the U.S.

As for me, today I am on the Mary Catherine, my namesake, in the Florida Keys heading in to have a couple of drinks later at Buried Money. I am exactly where I should be, right next to my Theo. Oh, and then there's Izzy, who decided to stow away. Oh well, can't have everything.

A NOTE TO THE READER

Dear Reader,

Thank you for reading my book. I hope you enjoyed reading it and I hope you would check out my other books. I would be most grateful if you would spread the word. In addition, I hope you would take a minute or two to post an honest review on Amazon. If you would like to chat, I would love to hear from you. Please email me at author@ritamoreau.com.

Drop in and say hello at www.ritamoreau.com
www.facebook.com/RitaMoreauAuthor
Until next time,

Rita

ACKNOWLEDGMENTS

Rita Moreau is the author of three novels and one novella. She lives in Florida with her husband, George, who brags to everyone that he is the author's husband. Without his motivation and help there would be no author.

I am very grateful to Alice Lawrence, Chairperson, Indian Shores Library Board of Directors, and the awesome volunteers of the Indian Shores Library. Thank you for your friendship and continued support.

Selected Bibliography

Briggs, Kenneth. *Double Crossed: Uncovering the Catholic Church's Betrayal of American Nuns.* New York: Doubleday, 2007.

Kramer, Jeffrey. *"Florida's Fabulous Treasures"* (March 2001)
http://www.pbchistoryonline.org/middle-school-lessons/031-Treasure/Florida-Treasure001.htm

http://www.treasurenet.com/forum/treasurehunting/messages/1008143.shtml

Made in the USA
Middletown, DE
21 May 2021

40184759R00176